Never Ask Why And Other Stories From the Romanoff Collection

Kezel Romanoff

Published by Grover Publishing, 2024.

NEVER ASK WHY AND OTHER STORIES FROM THE ROMANOFF COLLECTION

First edition. January 31, 2024.

Copyright © 2024 Kezel Romanoff.

ISBN: 979-8224832224

Written by Kezel Romanoff.

Table of Contents

For Mrs. Elwood, my eigth grade teacher who believed in me and had my first story published.

Never Ask Why

I HAD SURGERY ON MY shoulder not long ago. My bicep was massively bruised and the pain in my elbow was excruciating. The doctor concerned I might have a blood clot in my arm, ordered an ultra-sound of the full arm at the hospital.

Overbooked, the hospital's front desk, instead, sent me to the women's health clinic for the procedure. As I entered the empty clinic, the receptionist ushered me to the ultra-sound room right away.

As I settled into the oddly designed chair, the technician walked in and sat on her stool. She looked at me then her machine, "What did you do to your arm to require an ultra-sound?"

I looked at the middle-aged woman and blinked a few times, "I don't have my hearing aids in, you'll have to speak clearly."

She glanced at me as she turned a few nobs on her equipment, "I don't want to hear a whiny, it hurts, story. What did you do?"

I leaned back into the chair, "I was in my kayak fishing in the Columbia River and hooked a fish. I leaned over reaching for the fish, when a sea lion leaped out of the water after my fish. It missed the fish and grabbed my arm instead. With a mighty jerk the sea lion pulled my arm off and disappeared into the river."

"Upset that my favorite tattoo was on that arm, I was not about to let that creature get away with it. I grabbed my Bowie knife and dove in the river after it. Catching up with the sea lion halfway to the bottom, I cut one of its ears off. He hit me in the face with my own arm. I kicked him in the belly and sliced his other ear off. He let go of my arm. I snatched it before it could float away and swam to the surface."

"Gasping for air, I saw my kayak about a quarter mile downstream. I flopped onto my back, stuck my fingers in my mouth and did a one arm backstroke to the boat. Once I got into the kayak I took a hook and fishing line, and sewed my arm back on."

"It wasn't till I tried to paddle that I realized that I had sewn my arm on backwards. It took a while going in circles to finally get to the shore. When I did, I couldn't find my cell phone and had to walk over a mile to my truck just to drive myself here."

I took my arm out of the sling it was in and looked at her, "Boy, I tell you. Trying to shift gears with your arm on backwards is a challenge." I then dangled my arm out and wiggled it around as I glanced over at the technician. She had a strange look on her face.

Putting my arm down on the rest, I finished with, "Anyway the reason I'm here is the doctor wanted to make sure I didn't have a blood clot where the sea lion had bit down on my arm."

She blinked a few times trying to maintain a straight face, then squirted some gel on my arm. "I spent four years in the military police before switching jobs and coming here.... And that was the best damn excuse I've ever heard."

Here Kitty, Kitty

IN A BIG CITY LIKE LA, hundreds of missing person reports are filed every year. Many times there is nothing to them, or should I say the person in question disappeared to hide an affair from their spouse. Or the child wondered over to a friend's house. Many times however, the missing person ends up being found in the morgue. Either way, it's my job to find them. My name is Detective Joe Morgan and my partner is Sargent Harry Feldman. Together we work for the LAPD.

Arriving at my desk early Monday morning, I poured myself a cup of coffee and sat down to look over the new stack of reports that had landed on my desk during the weekend. As I thumbed through the pile, sorting them in rank of importance, I came across one that jumped out saying it was more than just a missing person case.

"Harry! I think we have a case here that could involve some foul play."

"What makes you think that Joe?" Harry said as he poured creamer into his coffee.

"A 23-year-old coed... boy, what a knockout picture. She hasn't been seen for three days. Her car was found in a seedy part of town. And, she doesn't answer her cell phone. It's the usual MO for a murder. Let's—"

"Whoa, don't jump the gun, Joe. Better let me see that file. You remember what the Captain said on that last missing coed case you went gung-ho about?"

"Yeah, but I was right... wasn't I? Drink your coffee and let's go, the case is getting colder by the minute."

Grabbing my jacket off the back of my chair, I badgered Harry to get moving out to the squad car. Taking my place in the driver seat, I drove slowly through the parking lot in order to give Harry enough time to read the file. Turning out the gate onto Rancho Boulevard, I punched the gas hard, squealing our tires and leaving a cloud of smoke.

Harry shook his head, looking at me. "You're going to get us fired Joe. What's up with doing that every time we leave the station?"

"Seen it on the television once. I think it's a great way to let the people of LA know we're on the job. Anyway, what school was that she went to?"

"One of those specialty colleges out on Azteca Avenue. But her car was found on Barber Boulevard, next to the Calico Tattoo parlor." Holding up a page from the file, Harry adjusted his glasses. "It says she was known to frequent the parlor. I'm for the parlor first, what do you think Joe?"

"Who filed the report, family or boyfriend?"

"Sorority sister... no boyfriend mentioned. The report says the girl's been back from deployment to Afghanistan for about a year. Oh, and no family. They died in a car crash while she was overseas."

"Wait... a... minute Harry. What did you say the name of that parlor was?"

"The... watch that red light coming up, Joe."

Flipping on the siren, I buzzed through the intersection.

Harry wiped his forehead and blinked his eyes as he spoke. "The Calico Tattoo."

Tapping the steering wheel with my finger, I glanced over at Harry. "You remember that case we did a few years ago? The one where a tattoo artist molested his clients? What was the name?"

"Don't remember Joe, but I do remember it was in the same part of town. Now do you mind slowing down."

"Vinnie. That's it! Vinnie Barboza, maybe we should pay him a visit."

"Good idea Joe. Maybe we should. In the mean time... do you mind?"

Vinnie's shop was in an old strip mall. Pulling into the parking lot, we rolled past a pawnshop, a Quickie Mart, a pizza joint, and something that resembled a secondhand junk store. All on one block, in a rundown residential neighborhood.

Getting out of the car, Harry leaned against the door, scanning the parking lot while I picked up the papers from his seat and skimmed through the report one more time. "What do you think Harry? Her car was parked in the far corner for three days."

"Don't know Joe. I see several security cameras covering the parking lot. No way anyone could have moved a body without being recorded. From their angles, I'd be inclined to say all of 'em covered the spot her car was in."

"I say we go pay Vinnie a visit first. Going through camera footage is such a pain in the butt. You coming Harry?"

Opening the parlor's front door and stepping in, we surprised the artist in question. The black-haired man was about 28, medium build, colorful sleeves on both arms. He looked up from his desk where he was drawing patterns. "Yes? Do you have an appointment?"

Flashing my badge, I stepped around the counter. "LAPD! We need to ask you some questions about a client of yours. Have you seen this girl before?"

The suspect made a fleeting glance at the photo before returning back to his drawings. "Nope."

"Look again Vinnie. Only this time pay a little more attention to the picture in my hand. My partner here, drank too much coffee this morning and has been having trouble with an uncontrollable twitch in his arm."

"Umm, let me see that picture again." Rubbing his chin, Vinnie studied the photo. "Umm, yea...ah, I think that's her. Yeah, I'm sure. I saw her three days ago pulling into the parking lot. I was standing in the doorway when she pulled in. I didn't see her get out of her car... that's when the alarm on the sterilizer went off and I turned around and came back in."

"I think you're feeding me a bunch of BS Vinnie. You don't really want me to send Harry next door to look at their security tapes, do you? If Harry has to sit there and watch one of those boring tapes, I'm gunna take you downtown until he's done. So, why don't you tell me what you remember."

"Okay. Okay, she came in and had some artwork done. There's no law against that!"

"Only if there was a little more than plain ink in the needle you used. Harry, did I ever tell you about Vinnie's first caper, while he was still in school? Isn't that where you got the name, Mad Dog? He used to do Quaaludes to relax his restless hands while putting flowers on the girls private parts. Only thing was, he'd pass out, or so he said, and do a face plant right onto the girls...ahem." Looking over at Harry, I shook my head. "Funny thing is, none of the girls filed a complaint. That was until he pulled it on the Mayor's 17-year-old daughter. What was it, Vinnie? Rape? Molesting a minor?"

"Damn it, Joe. I paid for that mistake more ways than I want to remember. Yes! Yes, that girl came in for several tattoos, but that's all!"

"Come on Vinnie, you're not telling us the whole story. I can see those veins sticking out on your neck, and your hands are twitching." Leaning against the counter, I folded my arms. "Harry, let me tell you what our brilliant friend here did after getting outta the joint? Seems every time a good-looking girl wanted a tattoo below the bikini line, methadone some how got mixed into the ink. By the time he was done, the girl would be unconscious."

"Is that so? I think maybe we should take him downtown, Joe. With traffic the way it is, we might have to take that route through the park."

"Hey, hold on guys." Vinnie jabbed his finger in the air at Joe, "You know that was a lie. Three of those girls admitted to jumping onto that wagon just to get a piece of the settlement. And, they admitted to never seeing me before. The other one was a consensual act, I gave it to her for the pain. I can't help it that in the middle of my work, she made the move..." he grinned, "on me."

"That's not what the DA said, Vinnie. Harry, cuff him while I call his probation officer."

"Hold on guys. If you take me in, I'll lose my license. Look, she came here two months ago and asked me to cover her with spots. She called them, 'her jaguar spots'. Up the back and sides of her neck, then around the ears and temples."

Harry tapped the counter with the cuffs in his hands. "Oooh, just like my favorite, that DAX on DS9?"

I glanced over at him. "What are you talking about?"

"Oh come on Joe, don't you ever watch TV? You know... Deep Space Nine. She was a Symbian. Carried another life form in the belly." Harry pointed the handcuffs at the artist. "I gotcha, Vinnie. What was so different about this one?"

"She wanted the spots to be iridescent. When I told her they didn't make ink like that, she pulled a small bag out from her bra and said to mix it into the ink." Vinnie held up his hand. "Hey! I know what you're thinking and it wasn't that way. I was curious, so I did it anyway. It made the most beautiful color I've ever seen. When I asked her what was in it, she snatched the bag from me muttering something about Mexican mushrooms and South American toads."

"You really expect me to believe that Vinnie? What do you think Harry? A repeat offense that went sour?"

"Sounds like it to me Joe. What'd you do with the body, Vinnie?"

"I didn't do anything with her." Squirming in his chair, Vinnie put his hands on top of his head. "I swear, it's the truth. I told her, no effing way I was going to do time again and she needed to put her shirt back on and leave."

"Did she?"

"No. She offered me a thousand bucks and said if I did a good job, there'd be more to come." Looking up at me, he raised his eyebrows. "Man, I tell you, that girl had a hard body like I've never worked on before. She must have worked out all the time, not an ounce of fat on her. Her tan skin blended perfectly with the spots." Covering his eyes with his hands, he sighed, "Laying on the table. Oh man, the canvass...DaVinci would have been jealous."

"What a sight, eh, Vinnie? A little too tempting? So, you added a little of your own juice into the cocktail. And she never knew, did she?"

"Up yours, Joe. When you gonna train this dude, Harry? It was nothing like that. It's like, I've never seen ink sparkle and change hues like that once it's applied. It was mesmerizing. When I finished, she got up, handed me the money and grabbed everything the ink had touched. I asked if she needed any help. You know... carrying everything out to her car. She shook her head, put it all in her bag and said she could take care of it herself."

"It was dark, and you let her go out there by herself?"

"I believed her, man. I mean, look at me Joe... six foot, two hundred fifty pounds. I ain't afraid of no one, but I definitely wouldn't want to meet her in a dark alley."

"Hear that Harry? Vinnie here is afraid to face a woman unless they're drugged."

"Shut up Joe. If your partner wasn't here... so help me, I'd knock your flippin teeth down your throat. You don't have anything on me, get out."

"Just a minute," Harry raised his hand. "Joe, I think I see some dots connecting. Vinnie, did she come back a second time?"

"Yeah, last month."

"When?"

"I don't remember the date, but I was standing out on the sidewalk watching the full moon rise over that dump of a tenement housing across the street. I was thinking of closing up early and going over to the bar; when she walked out of the shadows and came across the lot. Man... " Vinnie shook his head, "those spots were glistening in the moonlight. Made her look like a cat. You know, one of those kind you see in the video games with tight pants and shirt... long flowing hair, and a knife strapped to the leg"

Harry bumped my arm. "Love those games, don't you Joe?"

"What are you talking about Harry?"

"You need to get a life Joe, maybe you should've gotten married, had kids. Don't you think?"

"Watch it Harry, I'm still the one in charge. So she came back a second time, then what?"

"She said she wanted more spots. When I asked where, she said the entire belly and chest. I told her no, it'd take too long and I was closing. That's when she cuddled up to me offering two grand. That kind of money... I couldn't refuse." Vinnie point his finger at Harry, "But this time, I started asking questions while I was doin' the work. You know... something to take my mind off of what was in front of me."

"No, I don't know. Spell it out for me."

"Come on, Joe, you know; when you're working on a beautiful canvas like hers', sometimes it gets hard, too hard to work." Looking over at Harry, Vinnie shook his head. "Harry, he doesn't have a clue does he? You need to get a life Joe."

"Vinnie's right, Joe you definitely need to get out more."

"Anyway, the only way to keep my mind on the job was to talk to her. She said she was studying her ancestors' culture and that many of her ancestors were Jaguar warriors. I asked her why she chose that topic, and she got kind of indignant, then said that while in Afghanistan, she had captured twelve Taliban by herself, in a house her unit raided. Then, she captured another twelve on her own, during their next mission. I thought that was pretty cool and began to see her in a different light. That was, until she mentioned about Jaguars starting to visit her in her dreams and calling to her." Vinnie held out his hands and emphasized, "Hey, I get some real fruitcakes in here, but... wow, this was like right out of a comic book thing. Ya get me?"

"Harry, call DOD. See if you can get them to verify any of that and then call the VA hospital and see if she's in there."

"Sure thing, Joe."
"Go on, Vinnie."

"About that time I was getting up to her chest area... like I said, it was hard to stay on track with those thirty-eight C's staring me in the face. And I was managing to stay focused, but that's when things started getting a little weird."

"How do you mean?"

"She was laying there purring just like a damn cat. That was... until I wiped those mounds with alcohol and blew on 'em to make it evaporate faster. She grabbed me by my manhood and whispered, I'd better be careful."

"Your manhood, huh? You must have enjoyed that, you little pervert."

"Let's just say the sharpness of her claws kept me quite focused till the job was done. Then, like before... she got up, handed me the money, snatched the ink bottle from the tray and left. Didn't even put her shirt on this time. Hey! I followed her out the door trying to get her to cover up, but as soon as she walked into that moonlight... it was like she disappeared."

"Okay Vinnie. I'm getting tired of your BS. I'm pretty sure when we view the security tapes, they'll show you making her disappear into the trunk of your car."

"Hey Joe! DOD just confirmed what Vinnie said about the Taliban. Also said afterword's, she'd disappear for three nights during the full moon going on solo sorties into the villages. Got the village elders all stirred up. They claimed she would stalk through the village like a leopard."

"A leopard?"

"Yeah," Vinnie snapped his finger, "that's what she looked like, Joe. A leop...no...more like a jaguar!"

I rolled my eyes. "What about the hospital, Harry?"

Thumbing through his note pad, "The VA Hospital said she wasn't there. Also, I called her sorority sister. The one that filed the report. She gave the same story. Seems the girl would disappear during the full moon. Always came back in the morning tho, and never said anything."

"Full moon, eh? The moon was full yesterday. When was the last time you saw her, Vinnie?"

"I told you, a month ago."

"You're sweating, punk. I think you're lying to me. She comes to you on the full moon two months in a row. Yesterday was a full moon. I think if we look at those surveillance tapes, they'll say something different. Like, you saw her within the last three days. I'm right, ain't I, punk."

Vinnie looked away and shook his head. "Joe, you wouldn't believe me if I told you."

"Cuff the scum, Harry. A few days in the hole downtown, that'll convince him to come clean. Besides, I'm hungry and it's getting late."

"Hold on Joe, I'm not convinced he did anything. After speaking with DOD, I do believe she could whip the chump's ass and he knew it. So, when was the last time you did see her, Vinnie?"

"OK, OK. Last night. She came just before closing, wearing only a trench coat."

"Give me a break Vinnie, stop the fantasy crap. This isn't some computer game."

"I swear Harry! That's all she wore. I asked what she wanted this time and she said more spots, cover everything below the belt line. Then she took off the trench coat and laid down on the table." Reeling back in his chair and holding up his hands, Vinnie cocked his head. "Wait a minute, I know what you're thinking. I admit I had the same thoughts, too. That's why I grabbed a bottle of vodka out of the drawer and downed about a third of it. I needed something."

"So, creep. What stopped you from taking advantage of her this time?"

"Apparently you don't listen to your partner, do you, Joe? There's something odd about that girl. Like Harry said, she could have beat my ass silly. Anyway, the more spots I put on her, the stranger things became. I started around her ankles and tried talking with her again. You know, to figure out what was in that special mix she gives me. If I could figure out the formula, I'd be a millionaire. The best I could get outta her, she had just spent the last couple of days in Mexico gathering mushrooms and toads." Vinnie looked at Harry and shrugged his shoulders. "Anyway by the time I got to her knees she was purring like a damn cat again. It was spooky, kinda like I was in the Twilight Zone. But the more I listened to it, the more soothing it was. Kind of relaxing, you know. Then, maybe it was a little too relaxing. I made the mistake of reaching up out of habit and stroking her on her butt, like I would my own cat. That's when I felt it."

"OK, that's it. Cuff 'im Harry. We got his confession."

"Simmer down, Joe. Let's hear him out. Now, what'd you feel?"

Vinnie's eyes opened wide. "A tail."

"What do you mean a tail?"

"That's what I mean... a tail. Like on a cat!"

"You hear that, Harry? Like a cat's."

"You believe me, don't 'cha Harry? It was a small tail about a foot and a half long. When I lifted it up and looked at it, she spun around faster 'an lightning and had my wrist in her mouth. For a minute, I thought she was gunna take my arm off. After staring at me for what seemed forever, she let go and laid back down. Rolling onto her back she told me to hurry up." Looking at the floor, Vinnie rubbed his head. "I couldn't take it anymore. I grabbed a pill from my desk and had another drink."

"What'd I say, Harry? If we gave him enough rope—"

"No. I swear. It wasn't like that. As I got to doing the spots around her thighs, my hands were shaking something terrible and I started mumbling something about Jaguars. That's when I felt it tapping my back. I looked up... it was her tail! Only it had grown three feet longer."

"Oh criminey, Vinnie. How many of those pills did you take? Now, I suppose you're gonna tell me she climbed up in a tree and sat there with a big grin."

"I wouldn't know, Joe. When I saw that big tail, I jumped back and hit my head on the desk. When I came to, she was gone. The ink was gone... everything was gone. Everything but her raincoat. I still have it here in the desk drawer."

"Harry, let's get back to the station. I'm having a tough time believing this one. Maybe we should get him an appointment for the a rubber room over at the hospital."

"Sure thing, Joe. I'll take the coat, Vinnie, if you don't mind."

As the three of us were sitting in the car bathed with the light of the full moon, a dispatch came over the radio, "All units be on the lookout for a jaguar on the loose. Mugging victim claims a large cat looking like a jaguar, jumped out of the shadows and attacked the mugger. Once the mugger was subdued, it then ran away into the darkness."

One Stormy Night

IT WAS A DARK AND STORMY night and the two decided to put their differences aside to have a 'once and for all' discussion. Out of the rain, and with people around, they met at the local pub; a Werewolf and a Were-jaguar, blending in as they sat in a corner booth in their human forms.

Katerina, a Were-jaguar, sat on the bench with her back to the wall holding a vodka and cream in her hand. "OK, I'm here. What do you propose?"

Thaddeus, a werewolf, looked in his gin and tonic. "I...I know you won't like it. But, I think you need to give into your father's demands."

Katerina squinted at him through one eye as she licked the cream from her upper lip. "I should have known."

Thaddeus raised his hand. "Now wait a minute, hear me out please."

Giving the thought a deep sigh, she looked over at the bar. A burly man sitting on one of the stools, winked at her and blew her a kiss. Ignoring him, she looked back at Thaddeus. "Fine, tell me why."

He set his drink down. "The king paid me to instruct you in the various arts of defense. It's obvious that you don't want my help. And... Princess, there are other fish in the sea begging me to teach them."

Katerina snorted, "What are you talking about?"

Thaddeus reached over and tapped her hand as he cocked his head. "Your father wants a show. Then let's give—"

Katerina jerked her hand away from Thaddeus' as the burly man from the bar stepped next to the table. "No way." Looking up at the drunk standing beside her, she snarled, "What do you want?"

The man held out his arms. "It's me, Paul. You've come back."

Thaddeus stood up, pushing his chair back with his legs. "I think you're mistaken, we're new to the area. Now if you don't mind."

Katerina wrinkled her nose at the man. "I'm quite sure we've never met. How could anyone forget your repulsive odor."

Paul's muscles bulged as the knuckles on his clenched fists turned white. "Why are you talking to him?" He nodded towards Thaddeus.

The Werewolf offered his hand to Paul. "She said she's never met you, OK?"

Paul thumped Thaddeus on the chest with a large gnarly finger. "Stay out of this. This between me and my wife."

He grabbed Paul's wrist. "You're mistaken, sir. She's not your wife."

Katerina smiled at the drunk as she picked up her drink, waiting to see how this was going to play out.

Paul stared at the smaller hand on his, then sucker punched its owner. Turning to his 'wife', he latched onto her wrist. "Come on, Mary. We're going home."

The spots of Katerina's jaguar form began to appear on her neck and forehead as she sought to break free of his grip. "Let go of me, you pig."

Thaddeus rose up from the floor, where he had partially morphed into his wolf form. Growling, he bared his fangs.

"Be quiet woman." Paul backhanded Katerina, knocking her against the wall. With his other fist he tried to strike Thaddeus.

Katerina, with cat-like agility, leaped to her feet, pulling one of her daggers.

Thaddeus barked, "No, Katerina."

She hesitated for a moment, then with a sneering smile swung her weapon. The blade sliced Paul's shirt.

He looked down. The drooping material exposed a shallow cut across chest. Dropping his arms to his sides, he stared at the drops of blood slowly forming from the scratch. Suddenly, his eyes rolled into the back of his head and he crumpled to the floor.

Everyone in the pub stared at the duo as the two shook their heads while returning to their full human forms.

Thaddeus picked up his glass and downed the remainder of his gin and tonic in one swallow. "I think we better leave now."

Katerina looked at him in defiance as she slipped the dagger back into its sheath. "It was his choice."

The rumblings from the other patrons erupted into a roar when someone yelled, "She's killed Doctor Frankenstein's son."

"I didn't kill him," Katerina snorted.

Another patron jumped up, bellowing, "The doctor will take it out on us." A bottle came flying from the back of the pub and smashed on the table next to her and Thaddeus. At that, the barkeep shouted, "Someone grab the murderer."

Thaddeus pushed Katerina toward the exit. "Let's go, now."

Hurrying along the sidewalk with their heads down, they briskly walked the deserted streets in the rain, to the edge of town. The pair stood at the end of the sidewalk, looking around to see if anyone was watching. Satisfied that no one saw them, they followed a rutted footpath out onto the moors. From there they headed toward a shack on the cliffs above the ocean.

Thaddeus shook the rain off his coat as he stepped onto it's porch and opened the door. He lit the gas light while Katerina snatched a towel from its hook by the door and wiped herself down.

"Why did you have to do that," Thaddeus asked, as he knelt lighting the heater. "I could have solved the problem without upsetting the villagers."

"Oh really?" She threw her towel at him. "You were on the floor and that pig had his hand on me."

"That's exactly... arrgh," the match broke as he tried to strike it. "That's exactly what your father was talking about."

"I'm a princess." She asserted as she searched the kitchen for another towel. "And soon to be the Queen of our people." Katerina kicked an empty drawer shut. "Get me a towel."

"Get it yourself; I'm trying to get us some heat."

Standing next to the stove, she turned a few of the knobs on and off. "Does this thing work?"

"The striker's on the shelf. Try it," he said, still fiddling with the valve on the heater. "There, let's hope that's the problem."

When the heater began to glow, he stood up and looked to see what Katerina was up to. She had found a blanket and had wrapped it around her shoulders before putting a kettle of water on the stove. With the water heating, she took two cups from their hooks and set them on the counter.

Thaddeus smiled, "This is what I was talking about in the pub." He handed her the tin of tea from the table.

"What?" she asked as she took the whistling pot off the flame and poured some water into each cup.

"That he wouldn't—" Walking by him, she handed him a cup then sat on the sofa. "Know, whoa, ow, ow. Wow, that's hot." He juggled the cup between his hands. "I think he doesn't give you enough credit."

Katerina patted the sofa next to her. "Come sit and relax."

"I can't."

"Don't give me that garbage about royalty. Sit down."

"No. I can't, I'm soaked."

"You can share mine." She shook the edge of her blanket. "Or, you can get your own from the cot over there."

Thaddeus took off his wet outer garments and wrapped himself in a blanket. Retrieving his cup, he sat on the natty old sofa next to her.

She leaned her head on his shoulder and purred, "Thank you."

The pair sat in silence, drinking their tea while trying to get warm. Thaddeus stared at the flame in the heater, and Katerina softly purring, closed her eyes.

Opening her eyes, Katerina saw Thaddeus was no longer on the couch. She rose from the sofa and glanced around the shack. His cloths were gone and he was not inside. Opening the door, she called out his name, but the wind was so loud she could barely hear her own voice. Shutting the door, she went over by the heater and put her dry cloths back on. With the last button on her leather coat secured, she stepped out onto the porch in search of her mentor.

In the dim moonlight, she could see him down at the cliff, looking over the edge. Katerina stepped off the porch toward the path. In the middle of the yard, she could see the villager's torches across the moors as they headed in the direction of the shack.

In haste, she leaned into the wind sliding down the slick muddy trail toward Thaddeus. Struggling to stay upright as she ran screaming his name, the storm raged against her. Lowering her head, she ran the last dozen yards.

Within arm's length, Katerina reached out to touch his shoulder. As she did, she slipped in the mud, planting her head square into his back, knocking Thaddeus off the cliff. Landing on her stomach with her head hanging over the edge, Katerina could only watch and scream as Thaddeus hurled toward the sea below.

Then, through the howling darkness, she thought she had seen the green flash of his crystal orb. Pulling hers from it hidden pocket, she slid over the edge following his lead.

Checkmate

ONCE THERE WAS A KING ruling a large and fading realm. He yearned for the glorious days of old, but at the moment, playing chess and arresting protesters was all he could do to appease his desires. Even with that, he still felt he needed to do something to show the world that his kingdom was still powerful. Something that those around him would fear and respect.

Now, in this kingdom a young man who eyed the King with awe, thought the King was kind, generous, and that everything he did for the benefited the people. The youth watched every one of the King's televised videos and studied his ruler's writings fervently, hoping one day to become like him... a great leader of men!

The young man so enthusiastically supported their leader, that he wrote a letter expressing his own desires and asking the King for some advice. Proud of what he done, he told everyone he saw. The whole village laughed at him, knowing that the King would not respond.

Weeks later there came a response. A large, folded piece paper with the Royal Seal was delivered to him in the middle of the market place. Excited to show the King's benevolent side to all the scoffers, he carefully broke the seal. The letter had but one sentence... LEARN TO ~~WORK HARD~~ PLAY CHESS, IT WILL SET YOU FREE.

So elated to have gotten a response from his hero, he hung the paper on the wall of his family's hovel above where he slept, and immediately started learning how to play the game.

Many months later upon hearing that droves of the King's subjects were moving into neighboring countries, unhappy with his rule. Angry with their flight beyond his reach, the King blew up during a game of chess with one of his ministers. Swiping the board off the table, he sat back in his chair chewing on his fingernails. The minister, cautiously asked the King, "Has it occurred to you there might be a way to show the people that you really care for them."

The King snapped his fingers and jumped to his feet. "That's it."

The next day he invaded a smaller neighboring country. Seizing the portion where many of his former subjects had moved to. All the other countries and kingdoms around howled and hooted like a caucus of monkeys. But, alas, they did nothing otherwise... just as the King expected.

The young man, amazed at how the other nearby countries and kingdoms reacted, wrote the King once more. This time expressing, his awe at how the King pulled off such a feat in just ten days without drawing anyone else into the skirmish. Ending his letter stating his admiration of the King's leadership, he again asked for advice.

Impressed by the boy's letter, the King wrote back, saying the life of a King is like a game of chess, you never ask your opponent if you may move a piece. Move; counter move; check and mate. In closing, he wrote in bold letters; '**Speed and defiance in your moves, often confuse your opponent into making mistakes**'.

Quietly hanging the letter on the wall next to the first one, the young man nodded his head as he walked out of the family's shack and down into the open pit to dig coal with his younger brothers and sisters.

Once more the King became restless, wanting to flex his powers. His ministers, knowing their country could not afford another war no matter how short, quickly suggested that he host a series of games. Events that his countrymen excelled at, and a few that they didn't. This would show the world they were not some evil empire, but a powerful, and gracious, people. Smiling with the idea, he rose to his feet. "Losing a few and winning the majority, this would definitely boost my ratings among our people. Make it so."

The boy soon received a formal letter from the palace saying the King wanted all young men between fifteen and thirty to work on a stadium to be built next to the plaza. It was to be a coliseum where his country's glory would shine above all others. At the bottom of the paper, obscured by the King's signature, was a small disclaimer from the Finance Ministry stating;

Everyone will get paid the same generous five coins a day that they get in the coal mines. Also, in line with the King's benevolence, the Ministry will only ask for two of those five coins back in taxes, instead of the normal three. However, those who are wanting to work, must submit two coins to the Ministry of Labor each week. Remember, if you turn down this job, the King may frown upon you and your family.

The boy folded the letter, stuck it in his pocket and with a sigh said to his younger siblings, "For the King and motherland I will gladly work on this project." Turning and picking up Ivan, his pet snake, along with the milking jar he used to collect its venom which he sold to the doctors at the small hospital, the boy left for the plaza with his only belongings.

At the plaza, the young man was shown to his new home. The shack, made of rotting timbers and thread-bare canvas, was shared with other workers, and with mice coming out of the sewers looking for some place dry. It sat across the wide boulevard running along side the plaza and down in a ravine out of sight from the mansions and opulent apartments of the King's friends. Despite their inequities, the boy continued his raving that the King knew what was best for them.

As the work on the stadium progressed towards the final stages, they promoted the young man to lead a crew of tunnel rats, children who lived in the city's sewers, and dig by hand through the fractured rock to connect the old and new systems together. Reveling at the pay increase of a coin per day, he openly rebuked those who grumbled that the Labor Ministry now demanded three of those new coins in order for them to keep their jobs. "You should be happy to still have a job. Everyone else is being let go and have nothing."

Finally, with the stadium done, the invitations were sent out. When the runners and jumpers and throwers and skaters showed up the games began. It did not take long for the King to become upset, for the invited guests were winning far more games than the King had anticipated.

The young man, standing outside the coliseum with the others who were deemed unfit to be allowed in, listened to the games broadcast over loudspeakers. Watching the foreigners come and go and seeing the smiles on their faces, he asked one of them, "Surely your happiness is due to the gracious benevolence of our King, yes?"

The foreigner waved his hand in a wide arc as he replied, "Look around, your King and his cronies are corrupt. They take everything for themselves, forcing the people to sell whatever they have in order to survive." The stranger turned to walk away, but then turned back around and pressed a gold coin in the boy's hand. " Young man, the world outside of this kingdom has so much more to offer. Go see how other people live. Then ask yourself, is your King really benevolent."

Nodding, the boy graciously thanked the stranger.

Agitated with losing so many of the games and seeing it as a disgrace, the King decided to round up the usual protesters and dissidents. The Minister of Finance took the opportunity to point out their growing troubles with a neighboring mountain kingdom that had lots of gold. Slyly mentioning that if he did the roundup, the kingdom would not be able pay for the protection of his loyal subjects who procured his favorite cigars in a far, far away land. Let alone buy the caviar he so dearly craved, from the tiny coastal country of Lower Slobeanya.

Without hesitation the King puffed out his chest, snarling, "I know how to take care of that." The next day he sent troops and artillery into

Lower Slobeanya in pretense to protect his loyal subjects who worked on the boats.

All the neighboring countries again started howling, and raising a ruckus like a room full of monkeys. The King, smiled, knowing that's all they would do, and went about inspecting his new shipment of caviar.

Thinking of what the stranger had suggested, the boy wrote to the King once more, asking, in all his glorious wisdom why he would invade a smaller, weaker country?

To which the King responded; *One, as King I know what is best for the people; and two, their lives will be better under my protection and not under some elected group madmen. As one of my loyal subjects, you should know this already and had best not question him again.*

After reading the Kings letter, the boy quietly wadded it up, and threw it in the stove as he had no coal to heat his food. Turning to his pet snake, he picked up the milking glass and milked Evan before going to the market.

When no one formally challenged the King's move into Lower Slobeanya, the King then decided to show all the countries around, just how powerful he really was. For five days he planned to lead a parade of his mighty army around the capitol by day, and by night, he would be televised playing chess against any who could challenge him. Slamming his fist on the table after writing the decree, he shouted to his cronies, "Prepare for the festival."

On the first day, the troops stomped and sang as they circled the capital, while all of the King's subjects oohed and awed. Then that evening, several of the surrounding towns put forth their best players to challenge the King. After playing three challengers simultaneously and winning all three, the King stood stretching saying he was tired and hoped there would be better challengers the following night.

On next day the King brought out bigger war machines and more troops. Putting them through fancy maneuvers to impress everyone. Then in the evening, many of the further districts sent their finest players to challenge the King. Although it was a greater challenge playing five games at once, the King still won all five. While leaving the great hall and waving to the crowd, the King whispered to his ministers, "Find me a real challenge for tomorrow evening, or you may find yourself going for a ride in the woods."

When the boy heard of the ministers' search, he thought about the King's advice given to him several years ago. Looking around his shack, he picked up a pawn from the chess board in front of him and muttered, "Come Evan, let's indulge the King."

Arriving at the palace gate, he was told to go away as his kind were too far below the standards for entering into the King's presence. Pulling a folded paper from his coat pocket, he showed the guards his letters from the King. Unsure of what to do, they sent him to the Ministry of Defense. The Minister took one look at him and said as young as he is, how could he possibly pose a challenge to the King. Putting him on the stage would only serve to embarrass the King. The young man pressed back saying, "If the King really wants to show how kind and benevolent he is. Then, allowing me to challenge the King, would show his lower subjects that he cares for them."

Looking at the young man, the minister grabbed a Rook from the chess set on display in the hall and threw it at him. "Go home."

The boy did as he was told.

Once at home the boy took a black pawn and using his pocket knife, formed a sharp sliver protruding upward. Then along with the white King, he dropped the two chess pieces into the snake venom in the milking glass. Then, carefully removing the pieces from the liquid in the glass, he placed them on the window ledge. With his stomach growling, he took the glass and its contents down to the apothecary market, where he traded Evan's venom for a coin, in order to purchase a bowl of soup.

Giving the vendor back his empty bowl , the boy headed for his shack to collect the two chess pieces on the window sill, along with

Evan, before going to the palace once more. As he weaves his way amongst those favored enough to be involved with the pageantry, and those who are not, he sees the disparity between them. Sighing, he feels his pocket to make sure Evan is still with him. At the doors to the great hall, Security blocked his path and demands, "What are you doing here? Your kind are not allowed inside."

Holding out his letter from the King so that the Royal Seal could be clearly seen, he raised his voice for everyone to hear. "I am a Grand Master from the lowest of lower classes. The King has put forth a challenge. In a show of respect and unity of all classes, I accept his challenge."

The crowd waiting to get in, roared with laughter and mocked him. Security quickly ushered the young man to a table with a game board on it left from the night before. The guard pointed to the pieces in disarray and sneered, "While the King is giving his speech set up the board." Then as he turned to leave, chuckled, "That is if you know how."

Picking up the white King, he traded it with the one in his pocket. Carefully pulling out the black pawn from his pocket, he placed it on the square before the black queen. Taking a deep breath as he slowly pulled his hand away, he began to hum the national anthem while setting the rest of the board in its place.

Suddenly the curtains dividing the room began bouncing as a crowd the other side went wild. Walking towards the curtains to peek at the crowd, he was stopped by the Minister of Propaganda, who appeared out of nowhere and strode up to the table. "Young man..." he looked sternly at the boy, "these are the rules; The King plays the white side. When the King enters, you bow, and bow low. Do not annoy the King. Do not talk to the King. Never look him in the eyes. And the King always wins... Uhm...Let me rephrase that so you understand. You will let the King win, you understand, boy?"

The young man nodded as he bowed his head.

"Fine. Stay here and wait for the King. Do not leave your place beside this table."

Patiently the boy waited...and waited, while listening to the King's speech about the state of the country. About how the economy was booming and how those in the crowd will drown in their wealth. After the crowd quieted down, the King lowered his voice and proceeded to speak about giving this young man a chance to show his skills of chess and how the game produces great leaders in the military that is needed to serve the people. And as their leader, he is not afraid to be challenged.

Stifling a sigh, the boy tried to remain attentive, but the curtain opened as the boy did a little dance looking around for a restroom. The King ignored him as he walked by and abruptly sat down motioning the boy to do the same.

The boy bowed and whispered "May I use the restroom, sire? As I have made a poor call of judgment and will not be able to concentrate, giving you a noticeable unfair challenge".

With a look of annoyance the King waved the boy to go. Picking up the white King from the board, he started twirling it with his fingers. Soon the piece was in his mouth and he began biting on the crown as he contemplated his first move. Upon returning and seeing piece in the King's mouth, he hurriedly made his way to the table.

The King made his first move as the boy slid into his chair. Hesitantly, the boy slowly reach forth and moved the pawn in front of his Rook. Withdrawing his hand, he began to touch his pocket. The King grabbed his white knight and placed it several squares in front of the boy's queen. The boy stopped fingering his pocket, looked at the board for a moment, then carefully moved another pawn. The King, curling his nose as he leaped forward, deftly moved his bishop forward. Smiling, the boy reached forth and moved a third pawn forward, leaving his finger touching it as he studied his move. The King's face twitched and quivered the longer the young man left his finger on the pawn. Snatching his white rook the moment there was an air gap between the boy's finger and the pawn, the King slammed it down on the board.

Contemplating and moving slower than before, the boy reached in front of his black King, and moved its pawn forward. Before the boy could touch the time clock, the King snatched the boy's pawn replacing it with his white queen. He then slammed the pawn down to the side of the board, driving deep into his finger, the sliver the boy had made. "Che...eh...eh...eck," the King stammered as he formed a fist with his hand. His throat tightening, making it impossible to breath.

The young man reached across the board and knocked the white King over with his queen. "Checkmate."

Loud gasps and rumblings came from the crowd. The King fell forward, gripping his throat. Looking at the young man, he pleaded, "Hell...pha...me."

The boy calmly watched the King's eyes close as he pulled Evan from his pocket. He whispered to his pet snake, "I believe his words were...learn to play chess, it will set you free. And he was right my friend." The young man placed Evan on the floor at the King's feet. "Enjoy your freedom."

The Minister of Propaganda, quickly followed by security, surrounded the table pointing their guns at the boy. As they inspected the King for a pulse, Evan slithered across the Minister's foot, seeking the darkness in the leg of his trousers. "Snake," he screamed, jumping and kicking. Hysteria quickly spread with security and the people running in all directions.

Slipping behind the curtain, the young man walked away.

The Road to Morocco

THE SUNLIGHT REFLECTING off the yellow sand, burned Thaddeus's eyes, forcing him to keep them closed as he rocked back and forth. Trussed to the saddle on a large four-legged beast, he felt like a piece of luggage. His body ached from the fall through the doorway into this world. The only thing he could remember was hitting the sand, then tumbling down the sand dune in the dark before hitting one of these great beasts of burden as it lay sleeping.

He rubbed his eyes with his sleeve, then covering them with his hands, he looked around. Other than barren sand, the only thing to be seen was gray, human-like men with four arms walking beside their great beasts of burden. Many carried spears. Others had swords strapped to their backs, and the others that looked like they may have been their women, rode on top of the beasts. The single line of travelers went as far as his bindings would let his rise up and see.

Slumped over and tied to the saddle's horn, Thaddeus' back began to cramp. He tried sitting up, but the trusses were too tight and wouldn't allow it. He squirmed in an effort to stretch the ropes. As he moved, it change the rhythmic creaking of the saddle, alerting the beast's master that his captive was awake.

Thaddeus smiled at the gray man leading the beast. "I seem to be bound up. You wouldn't mind being a good chap and loosen these ropes for me, would you?"

Raising his spear, the seven foot tall man cut Thaddeus' bindings with its sharp metal point.

31

Thaddeus shook the bindings from his wrists and started to unwind the rope from around him. As the coils fell off, with his wolf like hearing, he became aware the only sound to be heard was the gentle creaking of the saddle. No wind, no one speaking, no birds cawing in the distance. He sat up and looked around. Without much thought, he grabbed the horn and started whistling a tune from an old movie that reminded him of the sand, called *The Road to Morocco*.

On the second verse, Thaddeus lifted his leg over the saddle and dropped to the ground. He strode up beside the tall traveler. "Where's this train headed, mister, if you don't mind me asking."

"Gack-ma-chi."

"OK." Thaddeus had to move fast to keep up with the tall stranger. "Where is this Gack-ma-chi?"

"Ahead, over horizon."

"Great. Say, you wouldn't have any water to drink?"

Using the butt of his spear, the man tapped one of the baskets strapped to his reptilian like beast of burden.

Thaddeus looked up at the basket out of his reach. Motioning with his hands, he asked, "You wouldn't mind... you know."

The traveler grabbed Thaddeus and hoisted him up onto the saddle. Surprised at the speed and strength of his new acquaintance, Thaddeus found himself clamoring to keep from falling off. "Not exactly what I meant, but thank you, my friend."

Lifting the top of the basket up, he saw several skin bags filled with liquid. "Mmm...are they all the same? I mean—"

"Same."

"You're not much for words, are you?" Thaddeus picked up one of the containers and pulled its cork. "Smells like water." He poured some into his mouth. "Tastes like water. Ugh, with a slight hint of... " he held the bag up and eyed it, "goat, I would say."

Putting the skin away in the basket, he leaned back first looking to his left, then to his right, he then stood up in the saddle. All he could see was flat sand and the long string of animals in the caravan as it stretched for miles. Sitting back down in the saddle he cradled his chin in his hand. "Say my friend, why are we going to Gack-ma-chi?"

"Required after harvest."

"Ah, the annual migration to pay taxes." Thaddeus quipped as he tapped the basket holding the water containers. "So I take it, everyone is carrying food to give to the king, yes?"

"No king. Give to Ra."

Thaddeus looked in the other baskets strapped to the saddle. "What did you grow? I only see skins of water."

"Yes."

"Yes what? Yes, I only have water, or, yes I have food?"

"Grow water."

Baffled, Thaddeus sat up straight in the saddle. "You're saying you grew the water?" He shook his finger at the man. "Oh no, no. I didn't fall from the sky yesterday."

"Yes you did."

"OK, you're right, I did fall from it. But everyone knows that water falls from the sky, too."

The gray man looked up at Thaddeus and shook his head. "Everyone knows water rises from sand."

Thaddeus thought about what the man said as he glanced around the sandy expanse. "OK. I take it, you gather water and trade it."

"Yes."

"Many of your people gather water, also?"

"Yes."

"Does anybody grow other things?"

"Yes."

Frustrated, Thaddeus blurted out, "Like what?"

"Patience."

Rolling his eyes at the answer, Thaddeus lifted his leg over the beast's back and dropped down to the ground. "Look, whatever your name is, I can't live off of water and patience. Do you have something to eat?"

The four-armed man reached into a pouch tied around his waist and retrieved a small bar of what looked like compressed seaweed. "Drink water with it."

Hungry as a wolf, Thaddeus bit off a chunk. "Ugh. Taste like sand."

"Of course. You need water." With two of his arms, he picked Thaddeus up and threw him on top of the beast. "Stay there till done."

Setting himself upright, Thaddeus hummed a few bars of, *Back in the saddle again*, as he popped the cork on a skin and drank some water. Suddenly, a multitude of flavors exploded across his tongue. Fascinated, he bit off another chunk, then quickly drank some water. This time, different flavors came and went like an abundant burst of fireworks.

When the 'fireworks' faded, he stuffed the rest of the bar in his mouth. As the bar dissolved, the results overwhelmed his senses in a kaleidoscope of colors, smells, and feelings of orgasmic proportions. The rocking motion of the beast enhanced the sensational effect as time became non-existent. Thaddeus' warrior senses told him to fight, but like a dog when its ears are scratched, he closed his eyes and laid across the saddle on his back, soaking up the sunshine.

The colorful sensations faded as he became aware of warm hands massaging his back. They felt smooth as silk as they rubbed the stiffness from his back and neck. That, along with the warmth of the stone table he lay on, encouraged Thaddeus to drift in and out of consciousness. All the while, the tall gray masseuse's second set of hands sharpened a knife.

His eyes still closed, he caught the whiff of a familiar scent. Taking a deep breath, he sighed, "Ahh, Katerina. You came to finish what you didn't succeed at on the cliff."

Pulling her daggers as she saw what was happening, Katerina waved them in front of the four-armed masseuse, forcing the gray creature against the wall. "That was not intentional. And right now," Katerina growled, "I'm saving your life. This priestess was about to sacrifice you."

Thaddeus sat up and yawned. "She was massaging my bruised back." Scratching the hair on the back of his head, he blinked his eyes trying focus on Katerina. "Throwing me off a cliff's not good enough, you have to kill the masseuse, too?"

Katerina stepped back lowering her weapons. "When I stepped through the doorway, it looked like you were about to be sacrificed on an altar."

"It is an altar," the masseuse boasted as she stepped forward and continued to work on Thaddeus's back. "This is a palace of pleasure and passion. We put everyone upon an altar."

The thinly clad masseuse motioned to one her assistants, who presented to Katerina a tray of the seaweed bars.

Katerina waved it away. "So if this a pleasure palace, how come there is no one else using its services?"

The priestess stopped massaging Thaddeus and glared at Katerina. "You need to leave."

The Were-jaguar's nose began to twitch as she partially morphed. She looked around at the Priestess' assistants. Their hands were on their own daggers hanging from their waists, as if they waited for the command.

Spying Thaddeus's sword hanging from a nearby candelabra, Katerina walked over and took it down. "I guess he won't need this anymore," she said, and slipped it over her shoulders onto her back. "I've always liked how the blade kept you from slouching." Flexing her back, she made the scabbard settle into place. Sauntering over to the Priestess, Katerina asked, "Do you mind?"

The Priestess's nostrils flared. "Go."

In one deft move, Katerina pulled the sword from its sheath and cut off the Priestess' head. Before the headless body could hit the floor, she pulled out her crystal orb, leaped upon the altar and straddled Thaddeus. Then with a flash of orange light, the two of them fell into the opened portal beneath them, and into a different world.

Take Me With You

THADDEUS SAT WITH HIS back to the wall in the corner coffee shop. His cup half full and his mind half empty. Sitting with his crystal orb in hand, he studied its polished surface. If he left his hand open too long, the orb would start to glow, casting a green aurora as it tried to open a doorway between worlds.

Finally bored with that while he waited for Katerina, he squeezed hand tightly around it and downed the last of his coffee. As he set the cup down, he saw the stranger that had quietly slipped into the chair across the table.

The stranger leaned forward with his arms on the table and whispered, "I'll give you one hundred gold crowns for that object in your hand."

Thaddeus stuffed the orb into its special zippered pocket in his leather jacket and sat back. "What makes you think I have anything?" He held up his empty hands. "Look for yourself."

The man rolled his eyes and leaned in closer. "You've been staring at your hand for the last twenty minutes."

Thaddeus shrugged. "I have a thorn stuck in my finger."

The stranger sat back. "Your hand was glowing green."

Thaddeus looked away. "You're annoying me, go away."

"I want the glowing thing you have," the man demanded.

Thaddeus glanced at the door, expecting Katerina to walk in, late as usual.

With persistence, the man placed five gold crowns on the table. "It's a lot of money for a toy."

"If it's a toy you want, there's a market down the street."

The man tapped the table with his finger. "I want that one."

Thaddeus snorted as he looked the stranger in the eye. "A minute ago, you offered me one hundred crowns. Why should I take five now."

The intruder slipped his hand inside his jacket. "My offer of a hundred was merely a figure of speech." The hair on the back of Thaddeus's neck stood up as he watched the stranger's hand slide from his jacket and place another coin on the table. "It was to get your attention before I give you my real offer."

With a sigh, Thaddeus signaled the waiter to bring him his bill, then cursed at himself for bringing the orb out in public. He knew better than to reveal it unless it was to be used. But he was bored waiting for her.

The man got to his feet and leaned on the table. "Give me the object, now."

Thaddeus glanced up at the intruder of his quiet morning. "I don't know what you're talking about."

"I know you're an off-worlder." The man jabbed his finger in the air towards Thaddeus. "That means you have a way or device to get off this godforsaken rock of a planet."

The door to the cafe swung open, Katerina stepped in. Glancing over at her, Thaddeus reached for the coins. The man quickly pulled a knife and pinned Thaddeus's sleeve to the table. "The shiny device first."

Unsure of what she had walked into, Katerina leaped onto the table in front of her, pulling both both of her daggers she did a somersault, landing on her feet next to the man. Placing a blade on each side of his neck, she bared her fangs hissing in his ear.

"Glad to see you could finally make it," Thaddeus said as he removed the man's hand from the knife pinning his sleeve to the table.

"What do you mean, finally?" She glared at him. "I've been across the street waiting for you."

Thaddeus chuckled as he pulled the knife loose from the table. "We talked about the clothing store, but decided on this cafe."

Katerina dropped her arms to her side and curled her lips. "We did not." The stranger reached over to pick up the coins. As he did, without looking Katerina placed the edge of a dagger on the back of the man's hand. "I distinctly remember telling you, the shop on the corner of Hellmier and Croanon."

Warily, the man gently tried to pick her blade up off his hand. "If you two don't mind, I'll collect my money and let you have a private moment together."

Thaddeus scooped up the six gold crowns. "I thought you wanted me to tell your future."

Katerina blinked. "What are you talking about?"

He put the coins in his pocket. "This gentleman thinks I have a crystal ball and offered to pay me one hundred crowns to tell his future."

The stranger winced as she pushed the keen edge of her dagger down harder on his hand. "A hundred crowns. You fool." She removed her blade from his hand and twirled its handle between her fingers before sheathing it. "Keep your money, he can't tell you anything. Including the time."

Rubbing the back of his hand, the man exclaimed, "I was about to retrieve my money when you stepped in."

Thaddeus winked at her. "I was in the process of telling him he was about to meet the most beautiful woman in the universe. Well worth his money to wait, I said."

Katerina folded her arms across her chest.

"Long dark hair, I said..."

She looked at the man. He shrugged and shook his head.

"A complexion smooth as silk, I said. A smile that—"

"Stuff it," she cut Thaddeus short. "Give him his money back."

"But."

Katerina's nostrils flared. "Give it back, now."

Hesitantly Thaddeus reached into his pocket and placed the coins on the table.

Katerina turned toward the door. "Now follow me across the street where you should have been."

Thaddeus rapped on the table with his knuckles. "Why? We're already here."

Whipping around, she snatched a half-full glass of water from the table and poured it into his lap. Then dropping the glass for him to catch, she spun around and stomped out the door.

The stranger picked up his coins. "My friend, let me give you some advice."

Thaddeus tossed the glass on the table. "What? Go chase after her?"

"No." The man shoved the napkin dispenser over to Thaddeus. "Leave this world and take me with you. It'll only get worse."

Thaddeus grabbed a handful of paper napkins and wiped at his pants. "What makes you think so?"

Putting five of the coins away, he took the sixth and flipped it in the air. "Once you no longer respond to their call like some pet, they'll hunt you down and make your life miserable." The coin landed on the table heads up.

Thaddeus took more napkins and pressed them to his pants. "No. She is most likely right."

The man picked up the coin and shook his head. "Trust me, it only gets worse."

Suddenly, the cafe door flew open and a large menacing figure of a woman filled the doorway yelling, "Harcore! Where have you been?"

The man cringed. "Quick, I'll give you a hundred gold crowns if you take me with you."

Thaddeus threw the wet napkins on the table. "I'm just going across the street."

The woman stepped inside and began ranting. "Harcore, do you know how long I've been looking for you while you sit here with your worthless friend? Why are you here, you should be at home chopping wood. Do you know how hard it is to make tea for my mother without enough firewood? Harcore, why don't you answer me?"

Harcore reached in his pocket and pulled out a handful of coins, "Here! Take everything I have, just take me with you."

"Harcore, why are you giving him that money? Harcore answer me."

Thaddeus stood up and took the money from the man's hand. "I see what you mean." Taking out his crystal orb, he held it up. A greenish doorway opened between the woman and Harcore.

She pointed a stubby finger at her husband. "No...you...don't!"

Thaddeus reached over snatching her hand, and jerked her into the portal after himself.

Harcore stared at the green light as it vanished behind his wife. In the silence that followed, he straightened his coat, then whistled a happy tune leaving the cafe.

An Ode to Country Living

LONG AGO I USED TO have a job that every man was envious of, and every woman blushed when I talked about it. Yep, in my younger days, just wearing that company jacket was a surefire pickup line in every bar I walked into. Cause on the back of that there jacket, embroidered in big bold letters, was the name of my business.....**Stanley's Stud Service.**

I know what yer a thinkin', but it wasn't about me. It was for my horse...my cow...my dog. You see, I grew up on a farm and early on developed a business plan for my retirement. Yes sir, bought me a young palomino stallion an' charged five hundred dollars for his service. Wasn't long, an' I bought a prized Hereford bull. Next, I picked up my dog, ol' Blue. He was a papered Blue Heeler. Then came a cat. Yes sir, a stud for every thing, that was my plan.

Well, my business was quite known in that parts of the state. Made me good enough money to marry a fine young outstanding woman. Along with a nice farm for raising kids, and room for my four-legged employees. Even made enough to buy a big fancy truck and trailer to haul them in.

Then one day after the birth of our sixth child, my wonderful wife said to me, "Stanley, it's time to rein it in, you can't be my stud no more. You're gunna have ta give it up."

Standing there dumb-founded, all I could do was stutter, "Wha',...wha'," as my crystal palace was a crumbling before me.

Laughing at the look on my face, she reached over with a smile, grabbed the belt holdin' up my Levis an' shook it. "No, darling, we have enough kids. It's time for you to get cut."

I fought back the terror at the thought of becoming a gelding, a steer,... a ... a. Not even the IRS can strike that much fear in the heart of a man. But, being the man that I am. The strong, macho, bronco busting stud that I am...I smiled and said, "Yes dear."

Oh that wonderful sweet wife of mine. She knew I couldn't make that call. So, right there in front of me, she picks up the phone and calls Doc Hewitt over in the town of Fox. When it came to explainin' to the Doc what the appointment was for, the two of them commenced a gigglin'. Soon the laughter that went over those phone wires. Had me too embarrassed to be in the room. Doing the only manly thing that I could think of, I went out and saddled up that there beautiful stallion in the barn and went for a long ride. Ah swear that horse could feel my pain.

Well...the day before the appointed, *cut off*, date. A registered letter came from Uncle Sam. It said that I missed paying last quarters' taxes for my employees. And if I didn't pay immediately, they would send an agent out to confiscate any assets... 'To Be Sold to Cover Your Debt.'

That sounds like the government. Thems not understandin' how you make a livin' an' taking away your livelihood just so's you can't pay. Crumplin' the letter, I threw it on dash board of my truck as I pulled away from the post office. Slowly, headin' for home, all I could think about was that one event about to befall on me.

Early in the morning on that fateful day, as I was a backing the truck up to the trailer, so's I could deliver Billy Bob, my prized bull, over to the Double X Ranch on the way, I glanced in the yard and seen Sammy the cat tail's a twitchin'. He was a gettin' ready ta pounce on a mouse, then all of a sudden a bald eagle swooped down a snatching poor Sammy in mid-pounce.

Bailin' outa the truck and grabbin' my rifle hanging in the rear window all in one move, all I could think was; *Those damn Revenuers. They ain't a lyin' when they sez they'll come a collectin'.*

Puttin' that there bird's tail in the cross hairs, I's a figurin' if I dusted his tail feathers he'd drop Sammy. Well... it didn't go that way. Seems the bird musta read my mind an' made a slight shift... an' let's just say Sammy ain't gonna suffer from anything that eagle's gunna do to him.

Shakin' my head in dismay, I turned to put the rifle back in the truck only to seen that I had forgotten to take it out of gear. That darned truck idled clear across the barnyard pushing the trailer right up against the barn doors. Countin' my blessings that it didn't smash through them doors, I shut the engine off, an' went about loadin' Billy Bob.

Yes sir, that there bull may be my number two employee, but he still hasn't figured out how to load himself up so's he can chase them girls around the pasture.

Anyways, as I was a untying the lead rope from Billy Bobs' halter, I seen ol' Blue, take off like a shot cross the yard towards the corral. Curious as to what got him so riled up, I stepped outta the trailer in time to see a big ol' cougar leap off the hay mound onta the back of my number one employee, Trigger, a palomino stallion. Racing round to the pickup, I grabbed that rifle, flung it over the hood and tried like hell to put them there cross hairs on that cat.

Hoo doggie! If you can imagine, that horse was a buckin' higher than any rodeo bronc I's ever a seen. Raisin' a whole lotta dust they were. I's could barely see Blue runnin' circles around Trigger's feet barkin' at that cat. My rifle was a goin' up... an' down... an'... up. I was a little hesitant squeezin' one off. Cause, I... you know... I didn't want to reach out and touch my horse like I did Sammy.

Gatherin' enough courage, I sucked in a deep breath an' began movin' that there rifle in rhythm with Trigger's bouncin'. Finally, I touched one off just as I was about to pass out.

That there cougar bailed off in a twirling leap. As he hit the ground, Blue grabbed holda his tail. Unfortunately, Trigger was a aimin' for the backside of that cat, too. But... as my luck would have it, he missed and struck ol' Blue, throwing that poor dog high into the air over the corral rails. That dang cat sure made a beeline for the timber. Didn't even stop by the hen house to grab a chicken dinner on his way.

By now, the wife was on the porch a hollerin' my name, askin what all the commotion was about. As I answered my wonderful wife, half the kids went running for the corral to check on their pets. An' the other half were a wailin' an' a cryin' around her feet.

Soon they reported that Blue was hurt, but alive. An' Trigger, was a all cut up from the cougar's claws. An' that he also had a big round hole in his left ear, which they were a certain was made by the cougar.

I didn't have the heart to mention Sammy.

With a sigh of relief, the wife said she would call the vet and take care of the animals. Then with a stern look on her face, she informed me that I was not to miss that there doctor appointment and pointed to my truck.

Noddin' an' lookin' at my watch, I figured I still had time to drop ol' Billy Bob off before making it to Doc Hewitts.

Then again, wouldn't you know it, in all that excitement I had forgotten to lock the kingpin on the fifth wheel hitch of the trailer. It made quite an impact when the trailer hit the ground. Poor Billy Bob, he refuses to go into that trailer any more.

After turnin' one mad bull outta the trailer, I went into the house and proceeded to tell the wife what a morning it's been, an' that, maybe I shouldn't go see the doc today. Being how my luck's been a goin' an all, you know.

What a sweet woman she is. She didn't say a word, just pointed towards the truck with a look that needed no explanation.

Arriving at the Doc's on time, I ambled in. The receptionist, she a started snickerin' at seein' me and says, "Here, let me take your jacket. Since you won't be needing it anymore."

Not givin' the comment much thought, I took my jacket off an' handed it to her. She held it up like a prize fighter running around the ring showin' off his trophy, all the while struggling to contain her laughter. At that point I caught a glimpse of a what she was a starin' at... the words, **Stanley's Stud Service**.

Oh the humiliation.

Sittin' in that there waitin' room, I was a beginnin' ta see my life pass before my eyes. Then ol' Doc Hewitt's voice retrieved me from the edge of the abyss. She had a wonderful voice that was soothing to listen to. Not to mention she was pleasant to look at, too.

Ol' Doc Hewitt was special to my family... see, we grew up together. She was my wife's older sister. Even took her to her high school prom. Don't know of another woman, sides the wife, that I'd trust holdin' a knife while my pants are down. She had an ability to use that sweet voice of hers' to distract you while she was a doin' her doctorin' thing on ya.

As I was a lyin' on that there table listening to her, I began ta feel my youth returnin' and in a moment of nostalgia, my hand slipped off the table onto her lap.

Suddenly I felt a sharp pain in the family jewels as Doc squealed, "Oops!"

My pride deflated, an' pale as a ghost, I dared ta raise my head an' see if my manhood was still intact. With a giggle she elbowed me, "I always wanted to pull that one on you, Stanley. Ever since that ride home after prom."

With a sigh of relief I lowered my head back down as the numbing effect of the sedative took hold and her soothing voice continued. "Your truck had the softest velour upholstery. You know it was the hottest topic in the girls locker room my senior year?"

As I lay there defeated, listening, but not caring, I began a looking for the silver lining... *Well... at least I'll still have'em, that's more than our steers can say.*

At that very moment, I heard a snap an' become aware of a tightening, strangling sorta feeling below my belt. Strugglin' with misplaced anxiety, I opened my eyes. My wife was a standin' next to the Doc with a big smile on her face an' a twirlin' in her hand, one of them there tools for placing them green rubber cheerios around a bull's testicles.

Wide eyed, I look at the two of them with a fear of uncertainty.

Unable to contain themselves no longer, they's a burst out laughing so hard they had to hold onto each other to keep from a fallin' on the floor.

What could I do with my pants still down aroun' my ankles, other than to give them a stare through my manly, steely eyes. Still a gigglin, the wife, she wiped the tears from her eyes, an' leaned over a kissin' me on the cheek and said "This is the happiest birthday I've ever had, Stud-ley."

Ah'll a never forget her birthday, again.

DAISY

IT HAS ALWAYS BEEN a question in man's mind whether animals and man could ever talk the same language. But to Max it didn't matter, his mule Daisy was his friend, companion, and confidant in their hardrock mine located under the desolate mountains. It was so far north, the Northern Lights were visible to the south and conversations with neighbors, could be weeks or months in between.

Max's neighbor, George, was a skinny as a rail transplant from a mega city down south. He was one of those vegetarians who often got their beard tangled with the bark of the trees he hugged. One of those who communed with nature, believing that man and beast were brothers, precious to each other's existence.

Around the first of each month Max would always make the long two day trek into the village to sell his gold and buy supplies for himself and Daisy. Stopping by George's homestead, about the halfway point between his mine and town, provided shelter along with a chance to remember how to talk with other humans before going into town.

As usual, upon his arrival, George tried convincing Max to 'free' Daisy.

"And what would Daisy do if I freed her?" Max asked.

George waved his arms out wide and grinned, "What ever she wanted."

"You mean like not helping me in the mine?" Max muttered as he undid the cinch around Daisy's belly

"Not if she didn't want to."

"But how would I get the ore out of the mine?" Max protested.

Helping lift the pack off the mule, George shot back, "Why can't you carry it."

By this point Max was shaking his head while filling her feed bag. As he hung it around Daisy's head he patted her neck and whispered, "There you go old girl, you're free now."

Looking at the ground, not being able to count the times this conversation had been repeated, he reached down plucking a bottle of whiskey from the pack and meandered towards George's cabin.

"Max you know that turning her loose like that, is not what I'm talking about. Animals are our brothers, not slaves. They have feelings and can communicate too," George tried to impress his feelings on his neighbor as he followed him into the cabin.

Max went straight to the table and poured two stiff drinks. Grabbing one, he pointed to the other. "Look at it this way George, Daisy is my friend and companion. We work together, live together... we even talk to each other and she never tries to pick a fight." Max poured himself another. "Shucks, what more could anyone ask for?"

"You know making Daisy go into that mine is unhealthy for her. And riding her into town is just another form of subjugation, it's humiliating for her," George snapped as he reached for the glass.

"Subto...Subta...Subagation? George whatcha talking about? I've never hurt that mule!" Max retorted.

George held the glass out, shaking it to emphasize his point. "No, no, I'm referring to slavery. Forcing another being to submit."

"Look here, young man. Daisy is a beast of burden. She was a put on this earth by God to serve man's need. And that's 'xactly what she's a doin.'" Holding his drink to his lips, Max slowly glanced around George's cooking area. Finally, tilting the cup and downing his drink, he continued, "However I think you been smoking too much of that wacky weed and not eating enough meat. How do you survive, not eating any meat?"

"That's exactly what I'm getting at!" George smiled as he wiped his mouth with his sleeve. "Animals are our brothers, eating them is cannibalism. This is their world as much as ours. To slaughter them, or enslave them... is so morally wrong. Did you know that corporate feedlots produce millions and millions of tons of methane gas. Which, by the way is melting the ice caps, and—"

"Whoa there George, you're gunna have a stroke if ya don't calm down. An' let me tell you, you don't want that to happen living out here all alone." Max poured another drink. "That there bicycle on the porch ain't gunna pack you to the hospital."

"You're right Max, I don't." George held up his hands in despair. "I came here to get away from all the injustices that humanity reeks of. It was to seek harmony and balance with Mother Earth." Sighing, he grabbed his pipe and began to fiddle with it.

"Tell you what George, let's go out on your porch while I eat my jerky and you smoke your herb. Then we'll talk about your garden instead of politics."

The next morning while putting his pack on Daisy, Max stopped long enough to remind George that the salmon are moving up the river and to watch out for bears.

"What do I have to worry about the bears for?" Clenching his fist, George recited his mantra to Max, "I don't hurt them, they don't hurt me, we are brothers," as Max bent down to pick up the bullet that had slipped through a hole in his pocket.

While bent over, a second one fell out of his shirt pocket striking Daisy's foot, spooking her into kicking at whatever it was that had hit her. Her hoof struck Max square in the head.

Reeling backwards, he stepped on a rake that flipped up smacking her on the hindquarter. Daisy took off down the path as Max wobbled around on his feet and stepped on the trailing pack rope. Coming to the knotted end, the rope jerked his feet out from under him and he landed on his back.

"Max! Max! Are you okay? Oh god, don't die on me Max!" George yelled as he tried dragging Max up onto the porch.

"Hang in there Max, I'm going to get Daisy so we can get you into town." Snatching his wooden walking stick from the porch, George ran down the path towards the river.

Spotting her on a tall grassy rise between the woods and the river, George raced over and grabbed her halter. Wheezing for breath as he stroked Daisy's forehead, he whispered, "Come back and help me take Max to the doctor in town." Taking hold of her lead rope he started walking back towards the cabin.

Digging in her heels Daisy, refused to move, all the while keeping her eyes and ears focused on the woods behind George.

George tugged on the rope. "Come on Daisy."

She didn't give in.

"Come on Daisy, please. We have to get back and help Max!" George begged, pulling harder on the reins.

Still staring at the trees behind George, Daisy laid back her ears.

"What do I need to do to convince you to help me with Max. He's not going to hurt you, he needs your help."

She didn't budge. George kicked her front foot. Daisy snorted, stepping on his. Wincing in pain, George swung his walking stick to get her off his foot, striking her on the ear.

"Stop it you fool," she bellowed.

Letting go of the rope and falling backwards, George hit the ground sputtering, "Did you just say something to me?" Jumping up and latching onto her halter, George shouted, "You can talk! I knew it! I knew animals could talk!"

"Shut up you fool," Daisy whispered. "There are bears just inside the trees. You want them to hear you?"

"What? How?" George stammered as he stepped back in excitement."I mean...how did Max teach you to speak?"

"Damn it, George, there are bears nearby. If you'll be quiet so they don't hear us, I'll tell you of the most guarded secret in the animal kingdom."

Raising his finger to his lips, George took a deep breath and nodded.

The mule looked him in the eye, then whispered, "When the earth was created, man and beast spoke the same language. And there was harmony in the garden. Then man decided to disobey the Creator. When that happened, man was cast out from the garden. The Creator then turned to the beasts saying it was forbidden to speak to man in his own language. And, because we all stood by complacent, watching him pick of the fruit, we must now serve him."

"No! No! That can't be," George shook his head. "Really how did Max teach you?"

"I'm telling you the truth," Daisy whispered.

"If that's the truth, then how come other animals don't talk?"

"I told you. It's forbidden. Now be quiet."

George clapped his hands and pointed at Daisy. "I knew it! Max is the one making you keep quiet."

Stomping her foot, Daisy exhorted, "The Creator has forbidden it. For those who speak to humans, it is punishable by death. Man and beast."

"Why?" George raised his voice and waved his arms. "No mother would harm her offspring. Least of all, Mother Earth!"

"George, ssshh!"

"The Creator! Bah...Max taught you to speak somehow, didn't he?" Pointing his walking stick at Daisy menacingly, George growled, "Oh man, you're just messing with me. If it's punishable by death, then why did you speak to me."

"It was a mistake. It just slipped out, as if I was with Max." Lowering her head, she sheepishly grins, "How about we just pretend you've had too much to smoke?"

"Augh!" George raised his stick, striking Daisy on the neck. "Too much to smoke...How dare you humiliate me. After all I've tried to do for you."

Screaming in pain, Daisy stumbled towards the woods trying to escape George's onslaught.

"Who's going to help you out here? There isn't, a soul around for miles," he yelled chasing after her.

"I am," a deep voice growled from behind George. Spinning around in surprise, he's confronted by a bear standing over 7 feet tall on its hind legs.

"Whoa... OK... Sorry, I kinda lost it a moment ago," George choked out. "Wait, you just said something." He pointed his stick at the bear. "I knew it. I knew if animals could talk, you'd say you're my brother and brothers don't hurt each other. I'm right, ain't I?"

"Could be, but I'm just doing my duty as directed by the Creator," the bear said dropping onto all four, slowly walking towards George.

"The Creator!" George yelled pounding his stick on the ground. "There is no Creator. There's just me... and you... and that damn mule trying to feed me some righteous story. Who taught you guys to talk? And don't give me that crap about a Creator and his rules."

"Okay" the bear politely grinned. "How about... uhh, prepare to meet your maker." Pouncing on the human, he grabbed George by the throat and shook him violently.

Dropping George's body to the ground, the bear spits out a mouthful of flesh. "Ugh, that tastes disgusting. I hate the taste of man's flesh, I'd rather eat rotting fis—"

Suddenly, a gunshot silences the bear and he slumps to the ground dead.

"Yes sir!" Max looked at the Ranger. "I got there just in time to see George take on that there bear. Trying to save Daisy, he was. Yes Sir! Real heroic I say. A bit foolish to attack a bear with a stick though. Don't know why he didn't take a rifle with him."

"Yeah, it was kind of stupid for him to do that," the Ranger agreed while finishing his report. " Well, thanks for bringing his body in Max, we'll notify his next of kin."

Stepping outside onto the street, Max picked up Daisy's reins, "Let's go girl, I can use a drink after that."

"Me too," Daisy whispered in his ear.

"Awe stop that Daisy, you know I don't take to women mumbling in my ear."

Brother Fox & Brother Rabbit

"I TELL YOU BROTHER Fox, if you don't learn to play that fiddle better, we'll never get enough money."

It's a violin, Brother Rabbit. And if you don't get rid of that machine gun, nobody will stop and listen."

"Never, Foxy, my friend. We need it for protection."

"From who?" Fox said as he laid the instrument in its case and looked around at the empty fields on both sides of the road. "Or should I say, from what?"

Rabbit, shoved his green bowler back on his head. "You never know Foxy. Them thieves like to jump outta nowhere to grab and run."

Fox rubbed the end of his snout then put on his glasses. "Yeah, sure. Have you looked around, the only thing in sight is this road sign." He knocked on the wooden post as he tried to read its faded words. "And I doubt—"

Suddenly, a bright green ball of light appeared in the air above the sign. Thaddeus fell from the glowing light onto the ground beside Fox. Katerina quickly followed him.

Fox leaped back. "What?"

Rabbit hollered, "I told ya, I told ya," as he jumped up and down pointing his machine gun at the crumpled duo laying on the ground.

Fox reached over and lifted the end of the gun-barrel toward the sky. "Put that thing away." Shoving his glasses back into place, he studied the pair. "Hmmm. I've never seen these kind of creatures before."

"I tell ya they're here to rob us," Rabbit roared, as he pointed the muzzle of his gun at Thaddeus and Katerina again. "Let me take care of them."

"No! Put that thing away Rabbit."

"Oh come on, let me take care of 'em."

"That's what you said about Mr. Chimps." Fox folded his arms and glared at Rabbit. "Remember? ...the farmer who offered us a ride into town."

"Hey, his wagon was empty." Rabbit threw the gun's sling over his shoulder. "It looked suspicious. Him going to market with an empty wagon."

Fox folded his glasses and put them away. "Don't be in a hurry next—"

Thaddeus moaned, "Oww, get off me."

Fox stepped back eyeing the duo. "They talk."

Katerina rose up on wobbly legs as she rubbed her head. "It was a good thing you went through first."

"Next time Princess," Thaddeus pushed himself up onto his hands and knees. "Give me a warning before you push."

Rabbit whipped the gun off his shoulder, pointing it at Katerina as she raised up to her full height. "Get back."

She was twice his size. Katerina snatched the gun from Rabbit's grip.

"Hey! Give it back."

"No! You're going to hurt somebody waving this thing around," she said holding the gun out of his reach.

Rabbit stomped toward Katerina swinging his furry fists as Thaddeus got to his feet and brushed the dust off his clothes.

Fox, looking at his broken violin case laying where Thaddeus had fallen, gasped, "Look what you did to my instrument."

"Sorry." Thaddeus held out his hand, "umm, my name is Thaddeus." He nodded at Katerina, "and she is Katerina."

"Pleasure to meet you both. I'm Brother Fox." He picked up his broken violin. "Now what are we going to do about this?"

"I think the issue... " Katerina stood there holding Rabbit's hat over his eyes as he swung his fists and kicked at her, "... is what are you going to do about this?"

"Brother Rabbit!" Fox dropped his arms to his sides. "Is that anyway to treat our guests?"

"Guests, smests. Thieves, I say."

Thaddeus pulled his sword and tapped Rabbit's belly with its broad side. "Rabbit stew, I'd say."

Rabbit stopped fighting and stepped away from Katerina. Shoving his bowler hat back, he began to dance around shadow boxing. "Put that pig-sticker down and I'll show you."

Thaddeus, pushing the tip of his sword in the ground, leaned on its hilt. "There wouldn't be a place around where we can get a bite to eat? Katerina and I are rather famished."

Fox smoothed the hair under his snout with his paw. "Eat, huh. There is a town just down the road." He looked over at Rabbit and winked. "We were just heading that way ourselves."

Katerina glancing over at Thaddeus, dropped the gun on the ground. "Good. I'm getting tired of eating roadkill."

Rabbit covered his mouth, gagging, while Fox shuttered, "Ooh, that's bad."

Katerina smiled. "No, that's good."

Fox looked up at her. "Why?"

"Because, rabbit stew would be mighty tasty, right now."

Rabbit backed away. "No it don't! It's bad for you."

"Why?" She looked at Fox. "Have you ever had any?"

Fox's eyes got big. He then quickly covered them and shook his head. "No! No! No!"

"Are you sure?" Katerina asked as she pulled out one of her daggers. "I'd hate to do something drastic for no reason."

"Now, now." Rabbit reached slowly for his gun with his foot. "Lets not do anything rash."

Thaddeus covered his mouth with his sleeve to hide his laughter.

"Why?" She looked over at Fox. "Have you ever had any?"

Fox shook his head.

Katerina slid her thumb along the dagger's blade. "Rats. The edge is dull and that's bad."

Fox uncovered his eyes. "Whew, that's good."

She held the blade out at arm's length, showing it to Fox. "No, it's bad."

Rabbit snatched up his rifle. "That's good for me." He pointed it at her and jerked on the trigger only to hear it make a clicking sound.

Fox gripped his violin tight to his chest. "Oh no. That's bad."

Katerina held out the bullets she had taken from Rabbits' gun. "Nope, it's good."

Fox wiped his brow, "Whew."

Rabbit, dropping the machine gun to his side, laid back his ears. "This is definitely going to be bad."

"Nope," Thaddeus chuckled as he put his sword in its sheath. Looking at Katerina, he shook his head, "It's going to be good, right?"

Rolling her eyes, she sheathed her dagger. "Oh, alright." Not yet finished toying around with Rabbit, she put her hand on her other dagger then bearing her fangs, she smirked, "This one's sharper."

Fox covered his eyes with his broken violin and started to shiver. "If you must, do it quick. I hate pain."

Rabbit sucked in a deep breath and threw out his chest. "I's never goes down without a fight!"

Thaddeus turned his back to them, choking on his laughter.

Katerina, with her hands on her hips glared at Rabbit, then in a flash wrapped her arms around him and planted a kiss on his furry cheek.

Sputtering, Rabbit pushed to get free from her grip. "Let go of me, madam."

Fox peeked from behind the violin.

Katerina bowed and kissed him on the nose.

Fox wiped his brow. "Whew."

Thaddeus put his arm around Katerina and held out his hand to Fox. "Come on, let's go to town."

As they turned to follow the path, Rabbit ran up and nudged Fox, "That's one baaaad girl."

The Old West

STEPPING THROUGH THE portal onto the muddy dirt street, Katerina slipped, falling hands down into the muck. Thaddeus reached to help her up as he stepped through, but just as he did, a cowboy racing his horse through the streets clipped him, knocking both of the travelers onto their bellies in the mud.

Jerking hard on the reins, the cowboy brought his horse to a halt and jumped off. "Here, let me help you. I must apologize ma'am for running into you." He reached over Thaddeus's back and pulled Katerina to her feet. "The muddy streets ain't no place for a lady."

Katerina glared at the cowboy as she wiped the mix of dirt and manure from her clothes.

"Why ma'am, I know just the place to take you to, to get cleaned up." Pulling his hat off, he pointed down the street. "Zora's spa for women folk. Here, let me help you." He took hold of her arm and escorted her to the wooden sidewalk.

Thaddeus, getting to his feet, wiped the muck from his clothes. "I have never—" The horse's whinny interrupted his rant, grabbing his attention. Totally focused on the magnificent animal, he didn't see the cowboy lead Katerina to Zara's place.

The horse stood still for Thaddeus as he stroked its neck. He had seen such marvelous beasts from afar, but never has he been so close as to touch one. Its smooth black hair covering the animal's rippling muscles, fascinated the werewolf.

The height at which a rider sits, must give him a commanding view over his enemies, Thaddeus thought as he stroked the horse's shoulder.

The animal snorted and shook its head as if it could read his thoughts. Thaddeus looked at the reins dangling down into the mud. He took hold of them glancing around for the animal's owner. Neither the cowboy, nor Katerina were to be seen. "I'm sure he wouldn't mind if I just sat up there and took in the view." Putting his foot in the stirrup and throwing a leg over the saddle, he sat gazing around like a general watching his troops. The horse stood perfectly still as Thaddeus raised up, standing in the stirrups. "Oh man. This would be something to ride into battle."

Suddenly, out of the corner of his eye, he saw a rock bounce off the horse's flank. The horse took off like a rocket. Galloping along the wooden sidewalk, it tried to brush its rider off on every support post along the boardwalk.

Thaddeus pulled hard on the reins as he kept yelling, "Stop...halt. I command you to stop."

The more Thaddeus hollered, the more the horse tried to throw its rider as it twisted and turned, and ducked into an alley, then out onto another street. When his rider didn't fall off, it barreled straight for a low-hanging sign. The thick, flat wooden board knocked Thaddeus out of the saddle, landing him on his back in a green-tinged mud puddle.

Free of its rider, the horse slowed to a walk and turned back into the alley, disappearing.

Sitting up, Thaddeus looked at the sign. It was solidly hung there advertising a bath house and laundry service. His face turned red as he heard the sound of a crowd gathering on the sidewalk, laughing and exchanging money.

Crawling to his feet, he sloshed through the muck towards the wooden sidewalk. At its edge he was greeted by a short, smartly dressed man who offered up his hand, helping Thaddeus onto the walk. "Good show. Good show. Come inside and get cleaned up."

Wiping at the muck on his shirt, Thaddeus read the sign next to the bathhouse door;

COLD BATHES 5 schillings
HOT BATHES 10 schillings
"I'm afraid I don't have that much money."

"Don't worry, the bath is on me." The man put his arm around Thaddeus, guiding him inside. "You've made me more money today, than I've made all week."

Greeted by the two laundry ladies waiting outside the private bathing room door, his new friend piped up, "Here you go my friend, leave your cloths outside the door and they'll take care of you."

Thaddeus hurriedly stripped and slipped into a hot tub of water. When the water cooled down and no one had brought fresh hot water to top off the tub, he sat up looking at the door. Noticing his sword and a few of his effects were not where he remembered leaving them. Thaddeus reached over and rubbed the wall; it was made of canvas.

Shaking his head in disgust that he hadn't been paying attention, he looked for a towel. Only to spot his undergarments, still rumpled on the floor where he had left them; and no towel.

Climbing out of the tub, Thaddeus grabbed his underwear to use them to dry with. Their stench made him reconsider. Instead, he threw them into the tub, along with a bar of soap.

Still wet and with nothing to dry himself, he went to the door. Peeking out, he spied a stack of towels down the hall. Thaddeus carefully left the door ajar and snuck toward them. Snatching one from the pile, he wrapped it around his waist, then grabbing a second, he threw it over his shoulders.

"Now to find my clothes," he muttered continuing down the hallway. Hearing an argument going on on the other side of a closed door, he paused. One of the voices sounded familiar, like the proprietor's voice. Thaddeus slowly opened the door. The proprietor and one of the wash-women were having a tug-of-war with his leather jacket.

Thaddeus stepped into the room. "Ahem. Is there an issue I need to know about?"

The proprietor let go of the jacket and smiled. "No, no. I was just about to bring you your clothes."

The wash woman snarled something in an unfamiliar language as she folded the jacket and placed it in a basket with the rest of his clothes. Taking hold of the basket, she walked over and handed it to him. "He try to steal your leather coat and pants."

Thaddeus reached into his jacket pocket. "Hmm, there was a gold coin in here." He looked at the proprietor, who at the moment, was trying to slip out the door un-noticed. "You know where it went?"

The man shrugged pointing at the woman.

Thaddeus grabbed his sword from a table next to proprietor and placed the tip against the man's ribs stopping him from leaving. They both looked at the wash woman.

She curled her nose. "Not me. He go through pockets before I wash."

Sheepishly, the man pulled the coin out of his vest pocket. "Oh, you mean this? I found it on the floor."

"Where's the green marble?"

The man started to shrug his shoulders, but then changed his mind and pulled that out of his pocket, too.

Thaddeus snatched them both. "You shouldn't steal from your customers. It's bad for business."

"He no own business. It's mine." The wash woman snapped and held up her hand, tapping her palm. "Ten schillings for bath and laundry."

Thaddeus leaned toward the man, sniffing. "I should have known, you don't smell like you would own a bath house." Nodding towards the woman, he growled, "You said it was on you, pay her the ten."

Pulling his trouser pockets inside out, the man whined, "I don't have—"

Thaddeus pushed on his sword.

"OK, OK." Reaching into his boot and pulling out two coins, the man lamented, "You can't blame a guy for trying to make a few schillings."

Just then the other wash woman came in the door. "Someone left these in tub."

"Those are mine," Thaddeus exclaimed as he lowered his sword and stepped back.

The two women made a few tongue clicks, whistles, and hand motions between themselves. Then the one with his wet undergarments shook her head in affirmation and hung his clothes above the stove.

During the distraction, the con-man slipped out the door.

Thaddeus, happy he got everything back, took a chair from the table in the corner and placed it close to the stove. With his outer garments at his feet and his sword across his lap, he leaned close to the stove to dry his hair. Ignoring him, the women went about washing more laundry.

His clothes finally dried, Thaddeus dressed and left the bath house searching for Katerina. Each street he walked was pretty much the same; a path of mud, lined on both sides with shops. Some had wooden sidewalks, others didn't. Searching around for her, he thought it odd that no one else was on the streets. The little berg-town seemed totally empty and deserted. Stepping from the dead-end alley, where he could hear cheering and yelling, like a game was going on in the back, he headed for the edge of town.

Rounding the corner of the last building in town, Thaddeus was greeted by the sight of the town's entire population gathered next to the stock pens sitting on the edge of the wide open prairie.

From where he stood, he could see a woman dressed in black, riding a black horse around and around the arena. Impressed with her handling of the magnificent beast, Thaddeus waded through the crowd.

Standing next to the corral railing, he threw his arms over the top rail, his jaw dropped as he saw Katerina riding the same horse that had ditched him earlier.

She was chasing some guy, trying to lasso him, while the town folks prevented his climbing over the fence. When the short muddy character ran close by, Thaddeus burst out laughing. It was the shyster who tried to steal his clothes. Lassoing him on her next try, Katerina dragged him into the middle of the pen beside a second bound figure squirming in the mud. It was the cowboy who escorted her to Zora's, and whose horse she rode upon.

Hog-tying the shyster, she jumped back on the horse, riding it round and around the corral, waving to the town folks as they cheered her on. The third time she passed Thaddeus, he called out her name.

Katerina jerked on the reins. The horse, reared up on its hind legs and clawed at the air. Jumping from the saddle onto the top railing of the fence as it reached full its height, she turned facing the crowd, bowed, then did a back-flip landing next to Thaddeus. "Whoooo, doggie! That was a whole lotta fun," she hollered and put her arms around him.

"I'll bet it was," Thaddeus said as he reached into his pocket. "What was it all about?"

"That worm thought he could have his way with me." She adjusted her leather jacket. "And that second slug, tried to steal my clothes. He's lucky I didn't cut his hand off when he reached under the tent wall."

Thaddeus grinned as he put his arm around her. "He nearly got mine, too." Opening his hand, he held up his crystal orb. Its green aurora grew, splitting the rowdy crowd that had began to encircle them. Stepping through, Thaddeus touched the first random portal they came to.

The doorway opened six feet above a grassy knoll. Falling through, they rolled down the hill laughing. Thaddeus lay there at the bottom waiting for the world to quit spinning, while Katerina, sat up sputtering and swiping at the spider-web clinging to her face. "What was that? He almost got yours?"

Thaddeus, rolling over onto his elbow, gazed over at her. "Ah, it doesn't matter." He took a deep breath. "You smell that? Bacon and eggs!"

The Butcher, the Boy, and the Dog

IN A NOT TOO DISTANT country, there was a local butcher named Ling. Times were tough and he struggled to make ends meet. Finding fresh animals for his shop was becoming tougher and tougher as wild packs of dogs were driving farmers farther and farther from the town, and its patchwork of houses. The more he asked the local authority to do something about the dogs, the more they ignored him, forcing Ling to turn to criminal elements to obtain his supplies.

Once down that road, Ling was forced to buy only from Mr. Lee, head of the local Tong. It wasn't long before Mr. Lee began to sell him sickly animals and charge premium prices for them.

Wang, Ling's son, seeing what kind of racket is going on, often tells his father not to pay their prices. Arguing, that what he is able to sell the meat for, barely gives them any money to live on. To which his father always quickly replied with the question, '*Where else can we obtain meat for our shop?*' And then tosses him a package for delivery.

Grumbling at his father's unwillingness to stand up against Mr. Lee, Wang would grab a knife from the rack on his way out the door to comfort his fear of the wild dogs while carrying the blood scented package.

Day after day, while passing through the dilapidated areas of the city, to tiny enclaves of houses, wild dogs would chase Wang, forcing him to run for high ground. Where he would slice off a small chunk of meat, and throw it as far as he could to distract the dogs. Many times the missing piece would often be noticed by the buyer, resulting in renegotiating the price. And, upon his return, Wang would confront his father as he handed him the money, "If you bought a bicycle, I could outrun the dogs and not have to haggle with the customer."

To which his father's response was always, "With what money, can we spare, to buy such a luxury?"

One warm, humid day after returning from his delivery, Wang began pestering his father again about the need for a bicycle. Having endured enough, his father picked up a large piece of meat, tossing it to his son, he says "Wrap that up and deliver it to the house at #5 Quoi du street for five Yuan and be quick. It will be supper time by the time you get back."

Wrapping up the meat and grabbing a knife, Wang ran out the door, through several polluted and weed choked fields. Around the abandoned mill, over a bridge that crossed a stagnant green flow of water, and into a small neighborhood of houses. Running up to #5, he lifted the heavy knocker on the door and let it drop. Slowly the door swung open, revealing an opulent interior, far more beautiful than anything Wang had ever seen.

"How much?"

The words brought Wang's gaze to the woman who opened the door.

"How much?" the woman asked again.

Looking at the house's decor, "Seven Yuan," he said.

The woman looked at the meat. "It's is only worth six and that is all I'm going to pay."

Pretending to grumble about taking a loss, Wang pocketed the six Yuan and headed home, exuberant that he and his father would be able to enjoy something extra for supper tonight.

Walking back, around the old abandoned mill, he noticed a hole in the fence. Thinking it would save time on getting home, he quickly ducked through the hole and jogged along a path through the piles of rubble. It did not take long before he realized he had made a mistake. His shirt had blood on it from where the package dripped on him and now he was in the middle of dog country. Grabbing the knife from his belt and gripping it tightly comforted him little as he skirted closely around the piles of rubble.

Rounding a mound of bricks, Wang, glanced cautiously about before running. Even then, he was hesitant whether to run or not.

Approaching a tall pile of debris, he looked up only to see the snarling teeth of a dog. Leaping at the same time as Wang raised his knife, the dog impales itself on the blade.

Trembling, he stood there looking at the dog. This was the first time he had killed something. Trying to think of what to do next, he hears the barking of other dogs coming closer. Hoisting the dead animal over his shoulder, he runs back to the butcher shop.

When he arrived, his father was not there. Looking around the dismal shop, Wang knew that he must do something to dispose of the dog, but what. He spots a family picture of some one wearing a fur coat. Looking at the picture and then the dog, he gets the idea of selling its hide to the tanner. Nearly complete with the task of skinning, an idea of cutting up the meat to distract the other dogs comes to him. Done with the job, Wang puts everything away and cleans up the shop.

The next morning, he enters the butcher shop prepared to explain about the extra meat, but is quickly ushered out the door with a larger than normal package. "Who is this for?" He asks.

"It is for Mr. Lee, master of the Tong. He asked for his tribute early this week. Lucky for us you brought that package back yesterday or we would not have had enough to fill his order."

"But father," Wang gasps, starting to tell his father about what had happened.

Ling pushes him out the door saying, "Hurry, hurry, you mustn't be late."

Walking down the street, Wang opened the package looking at the meat. It all looked the same. So he wrapped it back up and hurried on with his delivery.

On his way home to the butcher shop the sounds of barking dogs in the distance reminded him to inquire with the tanner about the dog's hide he had dropped off there.

Inspecting the pelt, the tanner says he would give Wang three Yuan for each hide like the one he brought in, as long as they are in good shape. Five, if the hair pattern is unique or the hair is long.

Stepping outside the shop, the young man hears the dogs barking once more, this time they are much closer. Picking up his pace, as he is not prepared to deal with wild animals at the moment, instead, he is thinking of what he could do with the extra money. The ringing bell of a man riding a bicycle with a tall load of paper startles Wang. Turning, he becomes enthralled at the sight. Suddenly, the growl from a dog that had been chasing the bicycle brings Wang back to reality. Gripping his knife and glaring at the dog, Wang keeps an eye on the creature as he reaches down feeling for a stone. Frustrated with not being able to find one, he breaks eye contact. The dog seizes the moment and leaps at the young man.

Swinging his knife wildly, Wang succeeds in crippling it. This time, he jumps on the dog, and holding it's head, he slices it's throat like his father had taught him. Standing up and taking in the situation before him, the young man now becomes aware of what to do with his new found money. Taking off his shirt and wrapping the dog's body in it, he tossed the whole thing over his shoulder and headed for the butcher shop.

Blending the meat into the shop's supply proved to be easy, but hiding the excess money from his father was challenging.

Several days later after delivering all his packages, Wang started wandering along the edges of the abandoned areas of the city looking for more lone dogs. He has found a single animal could be taken fairly easily, but he also knows, to take on a pack would be dangerous. Searching quietly, he spots a small brown dog drinking from a mud-puddle next to a pile of rubble that was once an old house.

Carefully picking his way around through the debris, trying to sneak up from behind, Wang leaps at the little Pug. Only to have it run into a hole in the rubble. Debating whether to dig into the pile, or let it go, he notices it's getting late and must go. For it is dangerous to be alone in the dark. On his way home, he convinced himself that using traps to catch dogs would be easier and faster than the way he's doing it now.

While gathering the parts for his traps, he finds a buyer who wants all the dog meat he can get, in another district of the city. Wang figures the long walk will be worth it, for in two weeks he should have enough money to buy a bicycle and then the long distance will become much easier and...profitable.

Finally, the day came when he was able to buy a bicycle. A black beauty, polished and shiny. Walking along side of it, Wang is hesitant to get on the machine. He has never ridden one before. Out, away from the crowded streets, he throws his leg over the bike and starts wobbling down the lane. Slowly, he gets the hang of it. Riding past the old house site, he rides by the pile of bricks. Again, that little brown Pug appears from nowhere, snarling at him.

This time Wang sees the white, fur patch in the shape of a star on the dog's back. Racing towards the dog, it disappears down a hole in the rubble. Jumping off the bicycle he points his finger at the hole, "Getting you will be worth it. Your star will make me rich." Placing several bricks over the hole, he whispers, "I will be back to get it."

The next morning, Wang tells his father he has bought a bicycle and now it will make their deliveries faster and safer. Also, they can now sell to farther away clients. His father wistfully nodded and laid a package before him asking, "How much did you borrow from Mr. Lee."

Wang spun on his heels grabbing the package and left, not wanting to get into an argument. Looking at the package when he got outside, *Mr. Lee,* was written on it. Not prepared to let Mr. Lee know about the bike yet, as it would mean having to pay a tribute for it right then, Wang took his time going to the Master of the Tong's house.

Arriving at the Master's house, he tried to hide the bike. But, Mr. Lee was standing in an upstairs window watching him. Turning to his minions, Mr. Lee says, "Bring the boy upstairs."

Ushered into the room, Wang is motioned to sit in a chair facing Mr. Lee. Quietly they sit there looking at each other. Finally pouring two cups of tea, Mr. Lee says, "I noticed the new bike you were riding, and I was wondering how much it cost? You see, I've been thinking my friends here could use several of them for delivery purposes. However business has been slow, lately, and I cannot justify such an expense."

Quickly assuring the Tong Master that they had been saving for years, Wang leaned forward accepting the cup offered to him. "In fact, business has improved enough in the two days that we have owned it," the boy glanced up into Mr. Lee's eyes, "father said he is going to increase his order from you."

Gazing at the boy while sipping his tea, Mr. Lee whispers, "He did, did he? Tell him I have another proposal for him. How would you like to deliver packages for me, also?"

Knowing to refuse Mr. Lee could be lethal, Wang slowly sips his tea while thinking of what to say. As he empties his cup he replies, "Venerable Sir, we have just obtained the bicycle and I am still learning how to ride it without dropping things. If I were to have one of your packages and dropped it, that would be a most tragic outcome for all." Wang bowed his head, looking at the floor, "If Mr. Lee would just give me some time to learn at my father's expense, then Mr. Lee would be much more satisfied with the results." Not waiting for a response Wang jumped to his feet, bowed to Mr. Lee walked towards the door; only to be stopped by one of the minions.

After a moment Mr. Lee motioned the thug to let him pass. "The boy maybe right."

Jumping on the bike and racing through empty neighborhoods to the pile of rubble he visited the night before, Wang removed the brick from the hole he had covered, placing a snare at the entrance. Then, finding a spot where he could keep an eye on the trap, he sat down looking around for more dogs. After several hours, the young man realized had been out smarted once more by the cursed dog.

Despite his effort to get that little Pug, it did not take long for Wang to prosper in his business of trapping and disposing of the feral dogs roaming among the abandoned factories. The tanner paid him well, and the meat supplier for that hamburger chain filled his pockets handsomely every time he made a delivery.

However, that little brown mongrel with the star kept eluding him. And, it wasn't long before Mr. Lee began noticing the shiny new items the poor butcher's son was acquiring.

Visiting Wang's father, Mr. Lee began to infer, "I see the butchering business had improved Mr. Ling. Maybe you should consider buying more Life Insurance."

Laying down his cleaver, the butcher calmly looked at the gangster standing before him. "Whatever gave you that idea? We can barely afford the animals that you sell me now."

"Come, come." Mr. Lee picked up a long slender knife, "Look at the new bicycle that Wang is riding." Holding it to his thumb inspecting its sharpness, he raised an eyebrow as he looked at the butcher, "And the new knives that he carries. Then there is the new shirt that he is wearing to the social club. Surely you are aware of this." Dropping the worn blade on the chopping block, Mr. Lee wipes his hands together. " It is as if your son has gone into business as a competitor to you."

Ling picked up his cleaver and slams it hard into the meat in front of him squirting blood onto Mr. Lee's hand. With a smile Mr. Lee leans forward wiping it off on the butcher's shirt. "Let's hope the next time we talk, that it is not your son's blood being wiped on your shirt."

Later that evening when Wang came home, his father confronted him about Mr. Lee's accusation, "Where is all the money you are spending coming from?"

Thinking it's time to tell his father, Wang begins explaining how he traps wild dogs and sells not only their fur, but also he's been selling the meat to a hamburger chain supplier. And has buried most of the money in a jar in the garden.

Very angry, Ling shouts at his son, "It is not worth your life to hide money from Mr. Lee. He will get it from you one way or another. You must take him his tribute before he decides to take all of this." He waves his hand around pointing to the butcher shop.

"It is not his money it's mine. I worked for it, not him." Wang yells back at his father.

Ling growls, pointing his finger at his son, "You will also offer to deliver his packages for him, too."

"I will not bow to him like you, father!" Wang yells as he grabs the door opening it. "I will make a name for myself, you'll see!"

Stepping out, he slams the door behind him. Jumping on his bike he rides towards the old run down factory knowing he could be alone there. Even though it is dusk, in his anger he feels that he is safe on his bicycle. As he rounds a pile of rubble, he spies the little white starred mongrel. Quickly picking up speed, Wang aims to run over the dog. Not moving, the Pug stands his ground growling until the bicycle tire is mere inches away. The mutt then steps aside revealing a piece of rebar which pierces the front wheel, throwing the boy over the handle bars head first onto a pile of bricks. Laying there dazed and wondering if he has broken any bones, Wang hears the faint growling of a dog. Slowly opening his eyes, he sees the Pug's face mere feet away snarling. Reaching down, Wang feels for his knife. Pulling it out, he painfully rolls over and stands up. Looking at the damaged bike and then the snarling little dog, Wang growls, "Ohh, you are mine now. And this time you will lose. Then, your hide will fetch me enough to leave town."

Standing his ground, the dog barks again. Suddenly the boy hears a second dog bark... then a third... then another. Glancing around, Wang sees he is surrounded by twenty of the little mongrels. Lowering his knife, the boy bows to the dog with the star on his back. "It looks like it is you, who has set the trap!" Then he lunged at the dog.

When Wang did not show up to pay his tribute, Mr. Lee claimed the boy had taken his money and ran away. The boy's father declared that was not true, but that, Mr. Lee had something to do with his son's disappearance.

Then, when the damaged bicycle was found days later, along with what looked like scuff marks of something big being dragged into a tunnel under the rubble, everyone had their own theory as to what happened to the young man.

The Dark House

THE HOUSE WAS DARK, even in the full light of day. Shrubs grew all around it, hiding most of the dwelling from the street. Dirty windows hid the pulled curtains from view. Broken wooden slates on the porch presented a danger getting to the door.

Thaddeus stood still, sniffing the air. There it was. Her scent once again. Ever since her prank at the coffee shop, her scent was etched into his mind. He knew she had to be here, but knowing that she was notorious for springing out of nowhere and challenging his prowess, he hesitated to climb the stairs.

"Katerina! I know you are in there. Come out."

A strange guttural voice from within the house bellowed, "Who are you?"

"It is I, Thaddeus."

"Go away. She's not here."

Her scent was faint. Thaddeus thought for a moment, *maybe the voice inside is right and Katerina has already left.*

Thaddeus turned toward the street to leave and noticed the twin full moons rising from the horizon. Seeing them, left an uncontrollable urge to morph into a werewolf. Unfamiliar with the inhabitants of this planet, Thaddeus knew it would be wise to get out of public view quickly before the moons' light, overpowers him. Glancing around, the only place to take refuge was the dilapidated house behind him.

Spinning around, he climbed the steps. At the top, her scent was strong once more. He drew his sword in preparation of one of her antics and carefully crossed the porch. "Katerina, I know you are in there. Open the door."

"I claim her by rights," the deep voice growled. "You shouldn't have taken her collar off."

"I don't know who you are, but you cannot own what is not yours." With that, the door gave way as Thaddeus put his shoulder to it.

Across the room, bound and gagged in a chair, was the Were-jaguar he was seeking. Thaddeus stepped inside and was immediately confronted by the owner of the gravelly voice; a tall female humanoid with the build of an Olympic weightlifter.

Thaddeus gripped his sword tighter. "By what right do you claim to own the king's daughter?"

The muscular figure picked up her mace that was leaning against the wall. "My people have no king." She took a step in his direction. "And I have clients that will pay handsomely for her."

Dodging the spikes on her weapon, Thaddeus swung his sword with all his might in an attempt to cut the wooden handle of her weapon in two. Twas to no avail. She was a master at fighting. Letting go of her weapon, she stepped on his foot before his blade struck its handle. When it did, she hammered his jaw with her fist, sending him sprawling.

As Thaddeus slid across the floor, his transformation into a werewolf became complete. Baring his fangs, he gave a low guttural growl.

His opponent picked up her mace. "I've heard of beings that can transform," she said as she brought her weapon down hard with two hands, missing his leg and striking the floor.

He rolled and jumped to his feet.

"Be still," she demanded. "When I get my collar on you, everyone will flock to my palace of treasures, just to touch the two of you."

At the sound of her words, Thaddeus stood up straight, lowering his sword. She swung her club at him. Sidestepping her swing, he moved closer to Katerina. Repeating the maneuver a second time, he this time got close enough to place the tip of his sword against the bound Were-jaguar's ribs. "Stop! Or I will kill her." He poked Katerina with its point. Her scream was muffled by her gag. Thaddeus glared at the muscular humanoid and declared, "She would rather die than be your slave. I am prepared to see that through for her."

The slaver laughed, "Ha, ha. Go ahead, kill her."

Reaching behind his back, he pulled a small dagger and cut the bindings holding Katerina to the chair. The last wrap of the coil pinched his blade. Thaddeus couldn't move fast enough to dodge the short spikes of the slaver's mace as they tore into his shoulder. He rolled across the floor howling in pain and losing his grip on his sword.

The slave master tossed a leather collar on the floor next to him. "Put it on. Dog."

The object of his rescue slipped the gag from her mouth. "Yes, Dog. Put it on."

Thaddeus lay there giving her that look of, 'Really? After all that I've done for you?'

The king's daughter slipped one arm over the back of her chair and answered him. "Oh, what have you done?" She crossed one leg over the other. "Killed me? No. Oh I know... rescued me?"

He sat up. "Yes, I was about to."

The slaver glared at Katerina. "Shut up, you over-grown cat. I'll deal with you later." Turning back to Thaddeus, she pointed her mace at the collar on the floor. "Put it on."

Katerina purred as she mimicked the demanding humanoid with one of her fingers. "Put the leather collar on. Mmmm."

Taking hold of the collar, he crouched in a kneeling position and fumbled with its hasp. With his sword several feet beyond his reach, he looked over at Katerina to see if she could render any assistance. She sat in her chair, licking her fingers and rubbing her ears with the back of her hand.

Thaddeus stopped. "Might I remind you, my dear lady, we are not free of this situation yet."

The slaver glanced over at Katerina. Grabbing the collar lying on the table next to the Were-jaguar's daggers, she flung it forcefully in Katerina's face. "Here's your necklace, my pretty. Put it on!"

Thaddeus, seizing the moment, leaped for his sword. He rolled to his feet as his hand gripped the hilt and in one motion thrust his weapon at the breast plate of his foe. She whipped up her mace knocking the blade aside. His momentum was too great and his sword penetrated through the wall, pulling his hand through with it. Like a monkey trap, each time he tried to pull free, the wall tightened its grip on his arm.

As he fought to free himself, Katerina leaped to her feet smarting from the sting of the leather collar hitting her. She grabbed her daggers from the table and swiftly thrust one high into her captor's back. Using that dagger, she leveraged herself up and cut the slaver's throat with her other. As her captor's body crumpled to the floor, Thaddeus stopped struggling and offered, "Well done."

Katerina wiped her blades clean on his shirt and put them away in their sheaths.

With his arm still stuck in the wall, Thaddeus waited until she finished adjusting her outfit. "My dear Katerina, would you be so kind as to go around to the other side of this wall and assist me?"

She looked coyly at him and stroked his cheek with her finger as she purred in his ear, "You? Need my help?"

"Don't." He jerked his head away and rubbed his ear on his shoulder. "Please, just go to the other side will you?"

Katerina rubbed up against his back and whispered, "My big protector needs my help?" She licked the back of his neck.

"Please, just go—" he shook his head to get her to stop.

Stepping away, "Fine, whatever you say, Teacher," Katerina slid her finger along the wall as she sauntered around the corner.

Thaddeus watched her step around the end of the wall.

On the other side, she pulled out her crystal orb, opened a portal and disappeared.

Seeing the bright flash of orange light reflect off the walls, he knew she had left him to fend for himself.

Bowl of Soup

KATERINA SAT STARING out the cafe window as she waited for her meal. *The staff in this restaurant moves slower than the seven year itch*, she thought as she glanced toward the kitchen, her stomach growling to be fed.

In the corner next to the kitchen door, sat a dark haired man with beady eyes staring at her. His eyes seemed to glow red every time she looked in his direction. He also didn't bother to divert his eyes and continued to stare at her when she glared back at him.

Tired of the game, she sat up straight, shook her long black trusses and tried to ignore him. After looking at everything in the restaurant, she gazed up into the mirror above the counter, and taking a sip of her tea, saw that the stranger hadn't moved. He was still staring at her. "Not my type," she whispered to herself. Putting her cup down, she grinned to herself, "But I think I'll toy with him till my soup shows up."

With her chin cupped in her hands, she looked over at him. Pursing her lips and and blowing him a kiss, she gave him a wink.

He didn't move, he didn't even bat an eye.

Katerina could have sworn that his dark black eyes glowed ruby red for a moment, then turned back to black. It was creepy, she thought as she looked away.

A movement outside the window caught her attention. Her view of whatever it was, was partially blocked by the curtain above the windowsill. Her feline curiosity quickly focused on the movement. She got up and patiently walked towards the window. It turned out to be nothing more than someone's abandoned jacket caught on a fire hydrant, its arms waving in the breeze. Katerina glanced at the stranger as she turned away from the window.

His eyes were still locked on her.

Keeping an eye on him in the periphery of her vision, she walked back to her table and made another attempt to elicit a reaction from him by blowing him an obvious kiss.

He didn't flinch and his stare seemed to intensify. Once more his eyes glowed deep red during the time she paid attention to him.

Unnerved, Katerina had never encountered someone whose stare could penetrate so deep down into her soul. Fidgeting in her chair, unsure if she should ignore him, or just go over and cut his head off for disrespecting her royalty.

Katerina folded her arms across her chest and turned her back to the stranger. She sat quietly pouting, facing the door, when silently, a waiter set her soup on the opposite side of the table and disappeared back into the kitchen before she could ask for some crackers.

Rolling her eyes in disgust, Katerina got up and walked over to a basket of bread sticks on the counter. She plucked three and turned around catching the stranger's eyes glowing iridescent ruby red. Agitated by his arrogant behavior, she placed a hand on the hilt of her dagger and bared her fangs. "I'm hungry and I don't want any problems from you."

His eyes went dark, and he still didn't move.

With the first spoonful of soup, Katerina began to relax and started to enjoy it's flavor. It was a kind she had never tasted before. And ordered it after overhearing several of the locals mentioning it had a flavor that was of a -to-die-for exquisiteness-.

By the fifth spoonful, she couldn't agree more. Even with that pervert and his glowing eyes staring at her.

A warm fuzzy feeling of contentment enveloped her by the time she got to the bottom of the bowl. So much so, that all she cared about, was those last few drops in the bottom. Not even the sound of the bell above the cafe door could draw her attention away from getting at them. Holding the bowl up to her face, she tried to lick it clean, and was completely unaware someone standing before her, calling her name. "Katerina. Katerina."

Satisfied, she set the bowl down. Her head, now bobbing back and forth, she tried to focus on picking up a napkin to wipe her mouth. With a deep breath of exhaustion, she fluidly planted her elbows on the table and cupped her chin with both hands.

Thaddeus pulled out a chair from the table and sat down. Katerina blurted out, "Oh! So you finally decided to come to me and apologize."

"What are you talking about? You're the one who disappeared."

Leaning forward, her eyes merely slits, she tried to rub her ear and missed. "I was hungry and you didn't want to come with me."

He picked up the bowl, waving it under his nose. "What did you eat?"

"Catnip soup."

Thaddeus put the bowl down with a smirk on his face, then picking up a menu. He slid his finger along its list of soups. Flinging it back onto the table, he started laughing, "There's no Catnip soup here. It must of been Cannabis soup."

"It was delicious, whatever it was." Her head slipped out of her hands and hit the table. She raised up slowly, glaring at Thaddeus through squinty eyes. "Why don't you have a bowl while I go deal with that creepy guy over there."

Thaddeus looked at the figure in the corner. "What about him?"

"He just been staring at me and won't talk. That's what."

Thaddeus slid forward on his chair and reached for her arm. "OK. It's time for you to go Katerina."

"Let go." She jerked away. "Not till I teach him some manners."

"Put your dagger away. You're not going to teach him anything."

She let go of the knife and leaned over the table. "So you think I'm not good enough to... to... to... ." She pressed her finger on the table. "Where was I going with that?"

"You were going out the door, taking a walk with me."

"Oh yes," she shook her head, "I was going to walk over and—"

"Nooo. You were going out the door with me."

Katerina stood up and flicked her hair over her shoulders. Sticking her nose in the air, she whispered, "As the king's daughter, you can't tell me what I can or cannot do."

Thaddeus put his arm around her shoulder. "This time I think I can. I don't think in your present state, you could teach anything to that old movie prop of Arnold."

Katerina pushed him away. "What are you talking about?"

Laughing Thaddeus waved his arm. "Look around you. Arnold owns this cafe. It is the only one of its kind on this planet. It was modeled after a Hollywood movie. That creepy guy over there... is an advertising prop for one of his movies."

Katerina looked hard at the decor for the first time since she had walked into the cafe. Giggling, she tumbled towards the door. By the time she got there, Katerina couldn't stop laughing and could barely walk.

Thaddeus took her arm. "Don't stop now, princess. Let's keep going."

Between bouts of uncontrollable giggling, Katerina barely managed to utter "OK," as she followed him out the door.

Arnold's eyes glowed red as he stood up and walked over to Katerina's table. His head jerkily moved from side to side as he took her bowl, placing it the tub with the other dirty dishes. Sitting back down, he snorted, "I shoulda listen to Maria and stayed in Hollywood."

When I'm 64

THADDEUS SAT IN THE coffee shop glancing at the old couple laughing and talking over their coffee. Taking out his time piece, he looked at the numbers. "Ten minutes late as usual."

Tucking the device back into his pocket, he glanced at the couple once more before staring out the window watching the traffic going by. Suddenly the traffic screeched to a halt and cars blew their horns at a lone figure dashing across the street. Thaddeus shook his head, guessing at who that person was as he gazed towards the door.

The figure entered the cafe. Sure enough, it was Katerina. Quietly sitting, he watched her brush the hair out of her face as she looked around the shop. Spying him, she smiled and strode over to where he sat.

Katerina, reached for an empty chair as the old lady by the window giggled out loud. The woman's gray haired companion reached across their table and rubbed her hands with his. Katerina stopped and stared at the two of them as the woman wiped a tear of laughter from her cheek.

"Umm, having trouble with the chair?" Thaddeus interupted.

His voice brought her attention back to him. Pulling out the chair she slid onto its seat. Smiling, she offered, "Sorry, got hung up in traffic."

Thaddeus smiled back and mimicked the old man by grabbing her hand. "What would you like to drink?"

The old lady's laughter echoed around the shop once more. Katerina nodded over at the couple. "What ever she's drinking."

"That's the only cup she's had since they came in."

"Then make mine a double," Katerina demanded as she rubbed her eyes. "After this morning, I need it."

Thaddeus got out of his chair and squeezed her shoulder. "Coming right up my Princess."

Katerina reached up touching his hand, then continued to watch the elderly couple flirt with each other.

Minutes later Thaddeus returned, placing a large cup in front of her and a smaller one for him, on the table. Katerina looked down at the mound of whipped cream, larger than the cup, floating on her coffee. "What's this?"

"You wanted double what she had; so that's what I got you."

"That's not what I meant." She sighed and slumped back in her chair. "Father said I have to come back for some formal meeting with the council."

Thaddeus, staring into his coffee, chirped, "You are the King's daughter, and you must—"

"Obey?" She folded her arms across her chest. "I'm tired of being a part of the royalty."

Thaddeus took a sip of his coffee, then set it down. "What is it you want?"

She eyed the couple again. "I don't know... something different."

"Katerina, look at me." Leaning forward he held her hand. "You know the curse of the Were-people. We don't age as the humans do."

Sniffing, she picked up her spoon dipping it into the froth. "I know. But it's... it's that they are so happy and—"

"And what? You're so miserable?"

She held a spoonful of the whipped cream aloft. "You don't have to be so blunt!"

"What word would you choose?"

Licking the spoon clean, Katerina raised her eyebrows. "I dunno. But not miserable. That's something the lower class become."

Thaddeus sat back. "Let's see, you don't want to be a Princess any more and only the lower class are miserable. What's that leave?"

Katerina scooped another spoonful of the cream. "I'm not sure."

Thaddeus snickered. "What?"

The old man laughed and hooted, "I remember that."

Katerina, with the spoon still in her mouth, turned her head to stare at the couple.

Thaddeus knocked on the table. "Kat, I'm over here trying to talk with you."

"What?"

"That's what I said."

Katerina picked up her coffee with both hands. "Honestly, Thad, you get so confusing at times."

Sighing, he rolled his eyes.

She took a sip, then slowly set her cup down. "All I want is to be wanted. Like she is, over there."

Thaddeus squeezed her hand. "You are wanted."

She blushed. "I know. But will you still want me when I'm sixty-four?"

He rubbed her hand and snickered, "You're way past sixty-four."

"I know. But will you still want me?"

Thaddeus smiled, "We are Were-people, we don't age."

Katerina pulled her hand back and wrapped it around her cup. "Yes I know, but will you still want me when I'm old?"

He gazed at her for a moment then picked up her spoon. Fiddling with it, he glanced out the window then at her. "You are already two hundred and fifty years old, Princess. And I have been with you neigh on half of those years."

She turned away and gazed at the old couple as she pondered, "But, will you still feed me?"

"Will I what?"

Katerina sat up straight, glaring at Thaddeus. "Will you still need me like he does her?"

"Katerina. We don't age like they do and our needs are different."

"Are you telling me you don't need me?"

"Of course I need you. But I'm merely stating the difference between them and us."

Katerina stood up knocking her chair backwards. "In other words I'm not important to you!"

"Of course you are." Thaddeus reached over to touch her hand as he spoke, "It's just that—"

The car's horn drowned out his words as it plowed through the shop's glass window. In the quiet as the debris settled, Katerina opened her eyes to see Thaddeus kneeling over her and wiping the dust from her face.

She smiled at him. "Are they OK?"

"Who?"

"The couple next to the window."

"They'll be together forever," Thaddeus assured her as he pulled his green orb from its hidden pocket.

Katerina turned her head and closed her eyes, letting a tear fall.

As the aurora from his orb enveloped them, Thaddeus whispered, "I hear your father calling us."

A Halloween to Forget

ON HALLOWEEN, I WENT to the dentist for a root canal. Grinning through a pair of vampire teeth that were part of his costume, he loaded me up on Novocaine so I wouldn't feel anything. After the procedure, and before he left the room, he clicked his fake teeth loudly as he warned me, "Now it's going to take awhile for the numbness to go away. Until then, don't drink or eat anything for the next few hours."

While struggling to get out of the chair, his assistant looked at me and offered her advice, "Remember, don't drink or eat anything until it wears off."

As I walked into the waiting room, one of the staff behind the counter warned me, "Be careful, sometimes that numbing agent may affect your eyes and how you see things."

Winking at her, I nodded, "Uh huh, yeah right. You're looking at someone who has a piece of metal in everyone of his teeth. Never had it happen."

Driving off to the grocery store, my phone rings as I pull into the parking lot. It was an old friend. We must have talked for an hour...OK, half an hour, before I told him my mouth was dry and my stomach was growling, I needed to go inside.

After hanging up I jumped out of the truck. That's when I noticed the world didn't quite seem right. Not a problem. When my stomach growled, nothing was right till it was satisfied. Walking rather briskly towards the automatic doors, they opened up as I expected. And, SMACK!

I walked into right into a glass door so clean, it was invisible. After rubbing my nose, I reached out to shove the door open, only to find there wasn't one. Steppin' forward once more, I hit that invisible barrier again.

Now I've heard some places have invisible glass ceilings. But invisible doors to not let me in? As I stood there trying to figure out what the problem was, I heard someone clearing their throat behind me. Steppin' aside I saw a post dividin' the entrance. "Dog gone glasses." I took 'em off and shoved 'em in my pocket. "They're suppose ta help, not be a pain."

Shakin' the dust off my feet, and my stomach growling something fierce, I made a beeline for the deli-section on the far-side of the store. I hadn't made it too far when I began noticing people were looking at me strange. Reachin' up and fingerin' my nose, "Ah yes, it's numb, but at least I don't feel any blood."

Stayin' on task, I picked up speed and nearly collided with a cart coming out of the soup aisle. The woman pushing it looked up at me, gasped, and covered her mouth as she spun her cart around and disappeared.

Snorting, all I could think of was she must of been laughing at the team logo on my shirt.

Then I locked eyes with the woman waiting at the checkout. She gasped and covered her eyes as she choked on whatever was in her mouth. I thought of grinning at her as I reached down an' checked my zipper. But what fun would that be if you feel if you're smiling.

Turnin' up by the ice cream freezers, I approached a mom with a couple of little-ones in her cart. Suddenly, the kids tried crawling out of the cart and into her arms. She screamed and slammed the freezer door, then I swear I saw smoke coming from her cart's wheels as she took off in the other direction. Wondering what her problem was I shrugged my shoulders and reached for the box of popsicles lying on the floor.

Looking for the handle on the freezer door to put 'em back, I couldn't find it. Seeing the one on the next door over, I turned to open it. That's when I saw the cardboard cut-out inside the freezer. "Boy, what an ugly lookin' thing. No wonder them kids were frightened."

Opening the door, I tossed the ice cream in then stuck my head in to get a better view of the cut-out. "Hmm, where'd it go?"

Letting the door swing shut, I caught a glimpse of the cardboard character hiding in the cooler once more. Snickering, "Its July an' they're already puttin' Halloween stuff out." I stepped back and got a full view of the character. Man that thing was ugly. Its eyeballs were all bloodshot, its lower eyelids a drooping down like they was a going to let them things pop out. Its exposed teeth looked like metal shrapnel stuck in its jaw. And its cheeks, wow! They...were...sagging, giving it a set of jowls bigger than my neighbor's Bloodhound. Not to mention it was drooling worse than the dog, too.

Reaching for my phone to take a picture of the thing, the glass door popped open from somebody slammin' another door further down. Strange, the cardboard figure disappeared until the door closed. Then it had a phone just like mine in its hands. That's when I realized that cardboard dude was my reflection. Jumpin' back and shrieking, I took off down the aisle.

Running to the meat coolers along the back wall. I grabbed the biggest, coldest slab of meat I could find and held it to my face. Ahhhh, I could feel the coolness on my face...and all the way down to my belly.

"Hey Mister. You can't eat that here, you have to pay for it first."

I lowered the package and turned to face the voice. "I'm not—-"

The young butcher screamed, "Gaww." And stumbled backwards over his cart. Jumping to his feet, he ran towards to front of the store screaming "Call the police! Call the police!"

"Well, that should've done something." Tossing the family size steak back into the display case, I looked up in the mirror at its top.

Besides that beautiful Halloween face staring down at me, now, there was blood all over my shirt, making me look like a ravaging zombie.

I heard a crowd heading my way. With no time to try another cold slab of meat in an effort to change my good looks, I ran for the door. Pausing just long enough to make sure there wasn't an invisible post in my way, I shoved the slow moving door out of the way.

Ducking around the corner, I slammed my back up along side the building waiting for the sounds of a lynch mob pouring through the entrance searching for their Frankenstein. Fortunate for me, no one came out. But as I looked across the parking lot trying to find my truck, a police cruiser with its lights on, pulled right behind it an' parked.

"Dang, how'd them boys figure out that's my truck?" Wiping my nose with my sleeve, I glanced around. "I'm gunna need someplace to hide for awhile."

Looking around, a few blocks down the road I see the dentist office I had left earlier. Covering my face with a hand I march off down the sidewalk. Not seeing the curb coming up, I tweaked my knee as I stumbled over it. Moaning, I limped along muttering, "This must be how Lon Chaney practiced for his role as the Mummy.

Getting to the dentist office, I peeked through the window beside the door. "Ah, no one around." Slippin' inside, I dropped into the first chair and held a magazine in front of my face. "I'll be safe, if I can just sit here till this stuff...wears...off..."

"Mr. Romanoff. Mr. Romanoff."

"What? Huh?"

"We are ready for you now."

Opening my eyes I saw the dental assistant standing in the doorway. Patting my face, everything felt normal. Taking a deep breath, I sighed.

She looked up from her chart. "Are you OK?"

Slowly rising to my feet I looked her square in the eyes, "We ain't using Novocaine today, are we?"

As the door loudly latched behind us, she winked. "This batch was specially made by me mummy." She held up a syringe the size of one used for turkey basting. "And its just for you."

"Argg, nooo." Twisting and thrashing about to escape her iron grip, I felt someone tapping my shoulder.

"Kezel, Kezel...wake up."

Groggily opening my eyes and stretching my jaw muscles, I rolled my head towards the movement to my side. It was the dentist peeling his gloves off as he was saying, "Now it's going to take awhile for the numbness to go away. Until then, don't drink or eat anything for the next few hours."

Holding my hand up, I ask, "Didn't you...I...umm..."

Grinning to expose his bloody fangs, he hissed, "Happy Halloween," as he handed me a piece of candy.

One for the Road

HAVING JOINED THE ARMY just as they were blending the sexes for Basic Training, many of the of the old guard Drill Instructors were unprepared for what to encounter. Trained to be a junkyard dog on the one hand, on the other, they were trained to be respectful to the fairer sex.

One day we were hauled out to a wooded area to conduct simulated war games. Standing in formation at the end of the day, preparing to load into "cattle trucks" for the ride back to the barracks, the Drill Instructor barked out, "If you need to use the facilities, do it now," and pointed to a few weather beaten porta-potties perched on the edge of the assembly area.

A handful of trainees dropped their gear and raced in a dead run for the privilege of being first; as the last one in line may not get the opportunity to use them. While the dust from the departed was settling, one rather tall lanky female recruit waved her raised hand trying to get her DI's attention while he was busy chatting with the other DIs. The more she waved her hand, the more he looked right through her as if she wasn't there.

When the last person finally returned to their place, the burly Sergeant turned to the young woman and, with a voice that would have cowered even the meanest dog, asked, "You got a question, maggot?"

"Yes sergeant. What do you do in real combat when you need to use the restroom?"

The Drill Instructor stood there for a moment glaring at the sincere young woman while the other Instructors turned away snickering, and the rest of the company cringed at the thought of doing push-ups because of a stupid question.

Softening his stance, he scratched the side of his nose and shuffled his feet in the dirt. He thought hard and quick before clasping his hat behind his back with both hands and softly said, "Sister, as the first bullet whistles past your head you'll piss your pants. And your asshole will pucker up so tight, for the next week you won't need that little square of paper that comes with your MREs."

The company stood muted in surprise at the DI's gentle response. But the Sergeant quickly regained control. "All right you maggots," he screamed, "drop and give me twenty while Private Jones here gets on the transport first."

Time to Practice

"KEEP YOUR STEPS SHORTER," Thaddeus said as he waved the point of his sword in Katerina's face.

She tapped the tip of his sword with one of her daggers. With the other, she hit the hilt of his weapon and swung around, exposing her back to him.

Thaddeus wrapped his arm around her neck, pulling her head back. "If this were real I would have taken your head off," he said as he nipped her ear.

Katerina leaned into his chest. "If this were real you would be minus your manhood." She tapped her second dagger on the inside of his thigh to emphasize her tactical advantage.

Releasing her, he pushed her away. "Touché."

She spun around, facing him. Shaking her long black trusses from her face, she sputtered, "Like I've said, you have nothing new to teach me."

Thaddeus lowered his sword and stood up straight. "That may be so, but I am doing what your father, our King, has commanded me to do."

"You did have to mention that." Katerina defiantly shoved her daggers into their sheaths at the reference to her father. "I'm done."

Without warning Thaddeus did a quick high step, followed by a round house kick to her shoulder.

She fell backward to the ground. "Ooff, that was uncalled for."

He waved the point of his sword at her. "A Were-jaguar must be prepared at all times."

Katerina raised her legs and arched her back, launching herself onto her feet. She pulled both daggers at the same time. "You son of a dog..." she snarled as she took a step to his right.

Thaddeus opened his fist, exposing the green crystal orb in his hand. "You're too late."

A doorway opened beside him.

"No!" Katerina sheathed her daggers and dove at him. "You're not getting away that easy."

Together they tumbled through the portal, toward an unknown destination.

Rolling through the space/time continuum, they fell out another doorway into a grassy meadow. As they lay there catching their breath, Thaddeus could hear yelling in the distance.

In an effort to stay prepared he decided he should pull another trick. Katerina kept an eye on him as he stood up.

Surprised, he twisted, deflecting an arrow with his sword. Katerina jumped to her feet and stepped behind his back, facing in the opposite direction. They had landed in a field between opposing armies racing toward one another in battle. Thaddeus quickly held out his orb and together they stepped into the portal as a volley of arrows whizzed over their heads.

Landing on a different planet, saltwater lapped at their feet while a cool breeze flowed through their hair. Together they scanned the nearby sand dunes. Katerina wasted no time, she jerked her elbow around, smashing Thaddeus hard in the chest. He reeled backward, losing his grip on his sword.

She snickered and quipped, "You have to be prepared, remember?"

Snatching up the weapon from the sand, she held it aloft admiring the blade. Grinning, she then waved the sharp tip in his face. "I have your weapon, so I've won."

He side stepped her move reaching for his weapon. "I haven't knelt, so no you have not."

She swung the heavy sword at him.

Thaddeus dodged the blade and continued to circle her.

She swung a second time.

Blocking her swing with his hard leather forearm shield, he grabbed the cross-guard, jerking the sword from her hands. She in turn, brought up her knee, striking the inside of his thigh and pushed him away.

Taking a deep breath, she put her hands on her hips. "I don't see how you can fight with that heavy thing."

Thaddeus, seeing what was about to happen took a step toward her and sunk the blade deep into the sand, giving him something to hang onto as he swung his legs out and wrapped them around Katerina's waist. She had no time to counter his move before a sneaker wave broke over her head from behind.

When their heads emerged from the receding water, Katerina sputtered, "So you do care."

Thaddeus got to his feet and put his sword away. "Nope." With water still draining from his clothing, he pulled out his crystal and opened a doorway. "It's more like, how would I explain your disappearance to your father, the king?"

"Not so fast." She reached out and grabbed his shirt. "You haven't knelt yet."

Thaddeus pulled the both of them through the portal, followed by a wall of water, washing them out the other side of the doorway, where they slid across the short green grass. Laying there, the sound of the car traffic was deafening. Thaddeus sat up. They were on an island in the middle of a freeway interchange.

Katerina tackled him, driving his back to the ground. She put her knees on his chest and grabbed his jacket collar. "Do you yield, peasant?"

"You haven't won yet." He took one of her daggers from its sheath and stabbed it in the ground. Using it for an anchor, he raised his legs and hooked one around her head, pulling her off him. Then reaching over he pinched her cheek. "And you will never defeat this werewolf."

Katerina pulled her other dagger and hammered his thigh with its pommel. Thaddeus howled in pain and rolled out of her reach. He ripped the other knife from the ground as he stood up.

Swing and dodge, swing and dodge, the two circled each other waving the daggers in the air, carrying on their practicing, oblivious to the slowing traffic around them. Thaddeus suddenly stopped, stood up straight, facing one of the freeways. Katerina lunged and swung her dagger. He dodged the blade and hooked her head with his hand, throwing her to the ground as he stared into the distance. "They're coming."

Katerina lay in the grass. "What do you hear?"

"Sirens."

She stood and sheathed her blades. "How far?"

Not waiting for his answer, she pulled out her crystal orb and put her arm around his waist. The doorway opened beneath them. Unsure of how or where they would land, she squeezed Thaddeus tight as the lights from doorways to other worlds flashed around them.

Finally, Thaddeus reached out and touched one. It opened and the two found themselves laying on top of a mound of hay in the middle of a pasture.

Thaddeus sighed and relaxed.

Katerina lay next to him in the warm sunshine and began to purr. After a few minutes she blew in his ear. "Do you yield?"

Thaddeus, deep asleep in the warm hay, didn't answer.

The Interview

A LOUD VOICE CAME FROM the other side of the heavy black curtain, "Welcome to our show, people. We are happy to have society's hottest two members as guests tonight. Please welcome the dynamic duo...... Thaddeus and Katerina!"

Katerina, stepping from behind the black curtain, raised both hands waving to the ecstatic crowd. Thaddeus, following, held up one hand and barely moved it.

John Levitt of the BBC's *Sunday Night* show, rose from behind his desk and held out his hand welcoming them. "Please sit. We're so glad to have you tonight."

Katerina gave him a hug and a peck on the cheek before sitting in the first chair, where she primped herself for the cameras while Thaddeus shook the host's hand then stepped around her to sit on the couch.

The crowd quieted down when John sat and raised his hands. "So, Katerina, Your Highness, I've been dying to have you on here for the last two years. And now you're here."

She reached over and patted his hand. "For tonight, you may call me, Katerina." She pulled her hand back and flicked her hair with her fingers. "Don't get any ideas, it's just for tonight."

Thaddeus rolled his eyes and shook his head as a drum roll came from the band on the side of the stage. Levitt looked at the camera giving it a sly grin. "Ooo... K." The host took a pencil from a cup on his desk and twirled it between his fingers as he glanced at his notes. "Ah...Thaddeus. Tell us how the most eligible bachelor was able to land the daughter of...ah... " Levitt lifted the top paper on the stack before him, "the King of the Were-People?"

Thaddeus, patting his knee, grinned. "It all started when I had a novel idea I called, *The Tango.*"

Katerina sat back and smirked, "That's another story."

"If I remember how it went, I had this idea. Wasn't sure how to work it, but... someone sent me a note offering to help. I was to meet them at the Acropolis Club. A novel place to meet I thought. So I went there.

"At the club, I remember standing on the edge of the dance floor looking for a staff member, so I could order a drink before sitting at my usual table. And there she was."

Levitt stopped fiddling with the pencil. "Katerina?"

"No. The waitress." Thaddeus scratched his nose with his knuckle. "She had set her tray down. Such a regal pose she had. And the gown she wore," he whistled. "That daring black dress enhanced her long black hair as it flowed over her bare shoulders."

"I've..." Levitt shook his head, "I've never been in that club. Are you talking about the waitress's dress?"

Katerina rolled her eyes and whipped her head backward with her mouth agape. "Nooo!"

Thaddeus smiled and pointed at Katerina. "She had on the most stunning dress I'd ever seen. Anyway to continue, the band had begun to play a tango and the movements of those dancering on the floor caught my attention."

Katerina started snapping her fingers and bobbing her head to an imaginary Latin tune.

Thaddeus chuckled, "Like I said, someone had written me a note, requesting I meet them there. I have a saying, business first. So I looked around." He began to rub his fingers together as he spoke. "But, she caught my attention once more."

Katerina smiled as she kept bobbing and weaving. The stage band quickly caught on to her moves and began playing a tune for her. Levitt raised his eyebrows and waved his pencil with the rhythm as he asked Thaddeus, "Her?"

Thaddeus gave him a sour look. "No. The waitress. She had my usual drink on her tray, a gin and tonic, shaken not stirred." Scratching his throat, Thaddeus crossed his legs and looked out at the audience. "Anyway, drink in hand, the music stopped and the floor thinned out enough for me to look over and make eye contact with Katerina. She sat there alone with her finger, ever so gently motioning for me to come over."

Katerina, still dancing in her chair, mimicked with her fingers what Thaddeus had just spoken of.

With his deep British voice, Thaddeus went on, "I cast my humbleness, aside and rose to my feet. Downing my drink, then shrugging my shoulders to settle my jacket, I started across the floor towards her. Halfway there, the band started to play a rumba... I couldn't help it. The hips began to sway. My feet were sashaying with the music. I had it down pat, and the whole time she sat there stone-faced, with her finger beckoning me." He slid forward to the edge of the couch. "As I stepped off the floor, still gyrating to the music, I held out my hand to her."

He stopped talking long enough to reach over and take a sip of water from his glass on the table. Katerina, still dancing in her chair, glanced over at him. "And?"

"And what?"

"Tell them the rest." She stopped bouncing around and took a sip from her own glass. "Or I will."

"Anyway," Thaddeus blushed, "her stunning beauty seemed familiar, but there was something about her eyes. They were lifeless, like an ancient doll, well-worn and frayed. I was confident it was the lighting in the room, so I stopped dancing, held out my hand once more and softly stomped one foot on the floor. She didn't flinch. Then I thought maybe it wasn't me she was looking at. I bent over to look closer into her eyes." He hesitated for a moment glancing over at Katerina. "With the flash of a coiled snake, she grabbed my shirt and jerked me closer. She threw her other arm around my head and stuck her icy cold lips to mine." Thaddeus had became very animated by now and pretended to wrestle with her once more.

"I tried to pull away. But I couldn't move. She had me at such an angle I was unable to fight." He mimed his arms being bound to his side. "Like a boa constrictor, she had me in her control. Then... the icy burn of her lips faded and was replaced by a soft warmth." He paused, looking at the camera. "Soon they were hot. At that point, I knew I had her under my control."

Katerina slapped his arm. "You did not. You were on your knees on the floor."

"It was out of respect for Your Highness."

"Oh, please." She reached for her water and took a drink, gargling loudly before swallowing. "I can still taste your tongue, yuck."

Levitt, mirroring her actions, had also picked up his coffee mug and took a drink. He choked at her last comment and covered his mouth to keep from spitting coffee on his papers. "Ha, ha. That reminds me, wasn't there something about a spell involved?"

"That witch said I needed to kiss a frog." Katerina wiped her mouth with her fingers and pretended to flick them at the floor. "And he was the closest thing I could find to one."

Thaddeus smirked, "Which witch would that be, the one on Sirus 3, or your mother?"

"The one you left me alone with, to fight by myself on Titus 9."

"I told you to say please, and you wouldn't."

"You left me there alone, you piece of—"

"Ahh." Thaddeus raised his finger. "If you remember, your father hired me to teach you—"

"And I told you, you were going to pay for what you did to me, if I had to follow you all over the Universe."

"Here we go again. You need to learn to respect—"

Katerina slid back in her chair, crossed her legs and folded her arms. "You're right, I have may have forgotten my manners, but—."

"Well." Cutting her short, Levitt picked up the stack of papers in front of him and tapped their bottom edges on his desk. "I understand the two of you have special powers. I mean the both of you are werewolves, right? What's that like?"

Katerina spit and hissed as she stared at the show's producer, avoiding the cameras. Thaddeus put his hand on her arm. "No, I'm a werewolf. Her Highness here, is a Were-jaguar."

Levitt looked at the crowd. "Sarr—ree! Your Highness."

"With the Were-People, only the men are wolves. The women are jaguars." Thaddeus rubbed her cheek with the back of his hand.

She jerked her head away. "We're warriors just the same."

"Cats, huh?" Levitt questioned.

"Yes," Thaddeus nodded. "A prank of nature you might say."

"I see." Levitt rubbed his fingertips together as he looked down at his notes. "What's it like working together?"

"Well..." Thaddeus took her hand and kissed it, "we fight like cats and dogs. But in the end the job gets done."

Levitt, staring into the camera, pointed toward his guests as he mouthed the words, "What a hoot."

Thaddeus sat stroking Katerina's hair and scratching her behind her ear as the producer egged the audience to laugh and clap at Levitt's comment. After they quieted down, the host leaned back in his chair. "Just what is it, that you two do?"

"Protect you humans," Katerina answered with her eyes closed and pushing her head against Thaddeus's hand.

"What?" Levitt chuckled. "I mean from what? Boredom? Space aliens? Oh I know...green tomatoes."

Thaddeus pulled his hand away from Katerina and glared at their host. Instantly she sank her fingernails into his leg as her head fell backwards. Letting out a howl, Thaddeus grabbed her hand. "Must you do that?"

Camera 1 zoomed in on Katerina's face if on cue, when Levitt grinned and sniped, "I must say, kissing a frog certainly didn't cure you."

Glaring at him, her fangs grew and spots became apparent on her forehead. Levitt stared back, curling his lips into a crude smile baring his teeth. "I also heard the two of you tore up the club because he stepped on your tail."

Thaddeus sat up straight. "That's not true. That's not what I told you backstage."

Katerina jumped to her feet, kicking the coffee table out of the way. "You told him what?"

Levitt shrugged. "That when you are fully transformed, you have a tail."

"Ooooh, how dare you!"

"What's wrong with what I said? That, your tail looks cute as it flicks from side to side."

"Cute!! I... I..." Her tail began to grow as she drew her arm back to strike Thaddeus.

Levitt grabbed her wrist. She turned on the host, hissing in his face. Holding up his cup of coffee, he smirked, "Here, use this."

Snatching the mug from Levitt's hand, she threw the coffee on Thaddeus. He jumped up, trying to pull his wet clothes away from his skin. "Ow, you...you still haven't learned."

"You couldn't teach a rooster how to crow," Katerina snarled, pulling her daggers. "Now stand still, you cur of a dog. I'm going to teach you how to squeal like a pig."

The two, now fully transformed into their Were-animal forms, squared off on the stage as Levitt stood waving for the cameras to come closer.

Thaddeus pulled his sword. Katerina took a swipe at him with her dagger, followed by a roundhouse kick. He smacked her backside with the flat of his blade. She let out a yowl and whipped around facing him in a squatted fighting stance. Thaddeus kept an eye on her tail as it twitched from side to side, knowing it would give him a split-second hint before she attacked.

Levitt shook his fist at the crowd. "Yes. There you have it folks. Has anyone seen a tail like that? And those fangs! I'd love to be their dentist."

The crowd roared and clapped as the host egged them on. Thaddeus straightened up and looked at the crowd. Katerina lunged at him. He twisted, dodging her dagger. Grabbing her, he pulled her in close. "We've been played."

The tension in her muscles relaxed slightly. "What are you talking about?"

"Look at that tail," Levitt yelled to the crowd. "Isn't it cute how it twitches? Swinging back and forth. And back and—"

Katerina spun on her heels, thrusting her dagger under Levitt's chin. "You slimy weasel. I ought to...but I won't. What should we do with him, Thad?"

Thaddeus shuddered as he transformed back into human form. Sliding his sword into its sheath on his back, he replied, "It's up to you my queen. Just remember, no blood."

"Hmmm." She stepped closer to Levitt, sniffing him, inches from his face. "Cut his tongue out? Eat him? No, that would mean shedding blood." She pulled away and used her second dagger to cut open his sports coat. "Mmmm, yes that's it, shed it."

Levitt smiled. "No problem." He took his coat off and held out for her.

Katerina shook her head. "Everything."

"What?"

"Everything." She pointed her blade at the band. "Play something."

The band stuck up the cliché striptease tune. Katerina poked him with her blade. Levitt began to disrobe. The crowd went wild, hooting and catcalling; this time egged on by Thaddeus.

Down to his undershorts, Levitt stopped and stood there with his hands to his side. Katerina raised her eyebrows and tapped his chin with her dagger. "All of it."

"No!" Levitt defiantly folded his arms across his chest. "This is as far as I go."

Katerina turned her head toward camera 1 and winked. Then with the tip of her second knife, she hooked his shorts cutting the elastic band allowing them to fall down around his ankles. Stepping back while keeping the point of her first blade under his chin, she faced the camera again. "Ooooh. What a cute little tail. Can it twitch from side to side?"

The audience burst out laughing and hooting.

Katerina raised her daggers above her head twirling them, before deftly shoving them into their sheaths.

Thaddeus stepped alongside her and put his arm around her waist. The crowd screamed for more. Instead, he held out his crystal orb.

The entire studio hushed as its green aurora grew, opening a doorway between worlds. Bowing to the audience, the dynamic duo stepped through and the doorway snapped shut.

A Scottish Night

THE TRAIN PULLED INTO the elevated station of, Glasgow Central. To get there the tracks cross the River Clyde, a smooth wide body of water that was studded with the remnants of shipyards from bygone years. I viewed the city out both sides of the train as it crept slowly along the aged rails to its platform. Out the window on the Eastern side, a fresh modern city shone brilliantly. To the west the city showed its age.

Before the train stopped commuters raced down the aisle of the coach, out the door and off the platform. My son and I waited for the crowd to thin before we stepped into the aisle. As we descended from the train and followed the last of the crowd, we marveled at the age of the station with its small pane glass walls. The stairs down to the street on the west side was of wrought iron, it too, caught our attention.

The walk was two blocks to our hotel, the Hotel Alexander. The walk soon revealed modernization had taken hold of the city on that side of the tracks. Just not our hotel, yet. It was a marvelous old theater that had been converted into a boarding facility when vaudeville disappeared into the shadows of time. Or it had been built as a dinner theater with a hotel above. I'm not sure which, because the heavy Scottish brogue of the clerk, was hard to understand as our host described the hotel's history while he checked us in.

A wide oak stairway that had the finish worn off, led us to our floor where we stepped from the landing into a narrow hall sparsely lit with small sconces that resembled candles. As we proceeded toward our room, the elegance of the raised red and golden velour wallpaper cried out for me to touch it. The floral pattern of the threadbare carpet exude a mystic awe of antiquity by itself. I could only imagine that this hallway could have been decorated before Oregon had became a state.

I relished my passage in this tunnel of time travel, until my nineteen year old son started getting antsy about his need to get into the room.

Unlocking the door to room 325, I stepped out his way and went to the hall window. The view from the fourth floor was essentially the street below and a ancient brown sandstone facade of the building across the street. The stone face was supported by steel girders that formed the backbone of a new building.

The setting sun lit the inner works of the structure and showed me not a soul was there. Thrilled I would be able to watch the construction during our stay I reigned in my excitement like a dog on a leash and stepped into our room only to pick my jaw off the floor.

The walls were bright blue. And the ceiling was a lighter blue with six inch wide white trim boards along the walls. Everything was trimmed with the wide boards. Doors, floor, windows, even the mirror on the wall behind the television.

The large baseboards and fourteen foot ceiling in the room, I expected. But, blue walls? It was not sky blue, it was the brightest true blue you could have imagined. Not only that, but the white trim was a pure white, not egg shell, or almond. The, blind you if you look directly at it, kind.

With a four letter word of disgust, I expressed my dismay of the color scheme to my son as he opened the door stepped from the loo. He rolled his eyes and informed me that the bathroom was a two-tone olive green with white tile around the tub. I threw my pack on my bed and moaned something to the effect that at least it was quiet.

At that moment the jack hammers across the street started their song. **Enough!** I snarled. I needed a cigarette and some exercise after the long train ride from London. With a jacket and the door key in hand I headed for the street.

My son chose the TV.

As I struggled with the heavy windowless wood doors to the street, I came to understand what the clerk had said of its need. When the hotel was built in the 1800's, two blocks from the waterfront, they were designed to keep drunk dock workers, inebriated sailors from the tall timbered schooners, and cold air off the river, from coming in. I put my shoulder against the door and pushed my way into the night

Outside, I looked down the dimly lit street with lights suspended above the cobblestone about every third block. Some were white, while others were yellow, casting an eerie glow. I chose to go farther west away from the train station.

As I walked along the street, fog rolled in. Formless wisps of the vapor swirled around windowless facades of the half-demolished buildings being renovated.

In my solitude, my mind drifted to a scene in the movie "Casablanca." I inhaled a puff from the cigarette that dangled from my lips. The cigarette begun to twitch nervously in a mimicry of Bogies' scene. I walked on with hands in my pockets. The clicking of my heels on the cobble stone echoed off the canyon like walls of the street, I wanted to avoid suspicion from prying eyes so I wrapped my imaginary trench coat tighter around me.

What I needed was a heavier one to keep the fog from seeping into my bones. While I walked and finished my smoke, I caught myself constantly looking up as if I expected to hear air raid sirens at any moment.

Suddenly I heard them; *Wheee-oooh, Wheee-oooh,* Air raid sirens! I threw my cigarette butt into the gutter. I looked fervently into the moonless night sky and scanned for the airplanes. Then I heard the loud thunderous echoing of metal slamming into metal. The lights of the city illuminated the fog, I couldn't see which way the planes were coming from.

The sirens grew louder; **_Wheee-oooh, Wheee-oooh._** Moisture begun to run down my face, confused as to what I should do. Then flashing blue light reflected off the windows of a building down the street. An ambulance screamed around the corner and onto the on-ramp to the M8 in the distance. As the wailing of the ambulance wanes the sound of train cars being coupled together echoes down the street from the train station.

I take a deep breath of the damp night air and turned around.

The fog lifted as I walked briskly toward the hotel and the bed that awaited me.

Also by Kezel Romanoff

BETRAYED
Pawns of Power
Betrayed The Eyes of the Tiger

Standalone
The Tales of Thaddeus and Katerina
He Stopped Loving Her Today
Never Ask Why And Other Stories From the Romanoff Collection